GONE WITH THE MIND

GONE
WITH THE
MIND

A Novel

MARK
LEYNER

Little, Brown and Company

New York   Boston   London

Little, Brown and Company
Hachette Book Group
1290 Avenue of the Americas, New York, NY 10104
littlebrown.com

First edition, March 2016

Little, Brown and Company is a division of Hachette Book Group, Inc. The Little, Brown name and logo are trademarks of Hachette Book Group, Inc.

The publisher is not responsible for websites (or their content) that are not owned by the publisher.

The Hachette Speakers Bureau provides a wide range of authors for speaking events. To find out more, go to hachettespeakersbureau.com or call (866) 376-6591.

Library of Congress Cataloging-in-Publication Data
Leyner, Mark.
  Gone with the mind / Mark Leyner. — First edition.
      pages ; cm
  ISBN 978-0-316-32325-3
  I. Title.
  PS3562.E99G66 2016
  813'.54—dc23   2015026139

10 9 8 7 6 5 4 3 2 1

RRD-C

Book designed by Marie Mundaca

Printed in the United States of America

GONE WITH THE MIND

PART I

INTRODUCTION

MARK'S MOTHER

Hello, my name is Muriel Leyner, and I'm coordinating director of the Nonfiction at the Food Court Reading Series here at the Woodcreek Plaza Mall. This series has been made possible by the generosity of the International Council of Shopping Centers and Douthat & Associates Properties. And I'd like to single out Jenny Schoenhals, the senior general manager at Woodcreek Plaza Mall, who has worked so diligently on providing us with such a commodious venue here at the food court, and without whom none of this would be possible. I see you couldn't make it tonight, but thank you so *very* much, Jenny, wherever you are. And last, but certainly not least, I'd like to thank our indispensable sponsors: Panda Express, Master Wok, Au Bon Pain, Auntie Anne's Pretzels, California Pizza Kitchen, Cinnabon,

Jamba Juice, KFC Express, McDonald's, Nathan's Famous, Sbarro, Subway, and Taco Bell.

Before I introduce our reader for tonight, I should point out that, because of the heavy rain and the flash-flood warnings that have been issued by the National Weather Service, no one—not one single person—has actually shown up for the reading...except, uh, I see that we've got some of the staff of Panda Express and Sbarro with us. I don't know if you two guys are just taking a break over there or are actually here for the reading...

PANDA EXPRESS WORKER

We're just taking a break. We're definitely not here for the reading!

MARK'S MOTHER

Well, welcome. There's nothing more dispiriting for a writer than to have traveled hundreds, sometimes thousands of miles to give a reading, and then find him- or herself facing rows of empty seats. So, I'm especially appreciative that you guys braved such inclement weather and at least showed up for work tonight. At least it provides the semblance of an audience.

"I've survived two assassination attempts: one on a

highway between Sophia and Plovdiv, Bulgaria, on November 11, 2006, and one in front of a hotel in Los Angeles on February 4, 2008. On December 3, 2012, I was raped by a robot on the corner of Fifth Avenue and 101st Street in New York City. In the summer of 2014, desperate for cash and back on crack, I sold the rights to my life story to a start-up indie video-game developer called MirRaj Entertainment (named after its founders, Miriam Rubenstein and Davesh Rajaratnam)." So begins *Gone with the Mind,* my son's autobiography, excerpts from which he will be reading tonight.

Mark Leyner was born at the Margaret Hague Maternity Hospital in Jersey City, New Jersey, on January 4, 1956. I was twenty-one years old. During my pregnancy, Mark's father (my ex-husband, Joel) and I were living in a one-bedroom apartment in a small brick building at 225 Union Street in Jersey City, between Bergen Avenue and the Boulevard. We paid, as I remember, fifty dollars a month in rent. I don't know why I remember all that so exactly…perhaps because it was our very first apartment. At any rate, about five or six weeks into the pregnancy, I began experiencing terrible, terrible morning sickness. Severe morning sickness. This was at the end of April in 1955. I would throw up all day and all night. (The medical term for this is *hyperemesis gravidarum.*) And I lost a significant amount of weight. I was down to something ridiculous like eighty-five pounds. My obstetrician-gynecologist, my *ob-gyn*—although we didn't abbreviate it back then—was a man named Dr.

Schneckendorf. This Dr. Schneckendorf, interestingly enough, had been my own mother's doctor when she gave birth to me in 1934. And he was a kindly old gent. But nobody really helped with the nausea. Most men, and I'd say *especially* doctors, looked on it as a form of self-indulgence. I valiantly tried to do everything humanly possible to keep it under control, but...people really thought of it as some sort of psychosomatic malady, almost like a form of malingering, as if I were simply this spoiled Jewish princess. That's the overwhelming feeling I got from most men, and certainly from most men in the medical profession at that time. At about three months, I began to "feel life," which is the expression we used then for a mother's first sensations of the fetus moving around in her uterus. And I could see an outline of his leg sticking out on my right side. He was a very high baby. And I remember being dismayed by what people said—that when you feel life, the nausea would abate—because that certainly didn't come to pass for me. I was going to NYU at the time—I was finishing up my sophomore year, I think. My father, at one point, had refused to continue paying for my school. He said to me, Well, you went and got married so young, and now you need to go out and work, and you and your husband need to take care of your own financial obligations; I'm not taking care of you anymore. So I went and got a job at a moving and storage company on Ocean Avenue in Jersey City, where I did billing and secretarial work. And I was *terrible* at it. Terrible! And I

went and told my father that I just couldn't stand being cooped up in that office on Ocean Avenue anymore,
and he relented and changed his mind and agreed to
help pay for NYU again. But it was very, very difficult
for me at that point, given how sick I was feeling just
about all the time, throwing up every single day, all day
long, and I was missing exams and I was taking Incom-
pletes, and I had no choice but to drop out, essentially.
But my husband and I wanted a baby very, very much,
and it was also a good time to get pregnant to protect
him from the draft—this was only a couple of years after the Korean War. So I tried the best I could to just
buck up and get through it. I kept a bowl cradled in
one arm to throw up in. I'd spend days at my mother
Harriet's house or she would come over to my house.
Afternoons were better, a little better, and I'd try to eat.
Chinese food—fried rice—seemed to set better in my
stomach. And Mark's father, after work, would stop at
the Jade, which was a Chinese restaurant in Journal
Square, and bring me cartons of fried rice. Whenever
I felt that I could actually eat something, actually keep
something down, I could be very peremptory about it. I
remember that summer being down at the Jersey shore,
at a beach club in Long Branch, and barking at my sister, Francis, "Get me a well-done hamburger and fries,
now!" because I knew how fleeting that appetite could
be, and I was absolutely determined to try to stay as
healthy and as strong as I possibly could for this baby
inside me. That summer we were staying at these lit-

tle apartments in West Long Branch. There were lots of Jersey City people. And almost every day, the men would go out on fishing boats. And there were rough seas out there. And later in the afternoon, when these guys would get off the boats, they were green, staggering. And I'd say, "Dr. Rubenstein, Uncle Harry, what happened?" I was a fresh kid. I had a fresh mouth. "Uncle This and Uncle That, what happened out there? You don't look so good." The fact that they were so seasick, so nauseous, delighted me to no end. Because as far as they were concerned, my terrible, relentless nausea was all in my mind. "If you kept yourself busy. Maybe if you had more floors to wash." They were all such imperious chauvinists. "If you continue this, we're going to have to put you in the hospital and feed you intravenously." Believe me, if this were an ailment of men's testicles, they would have found a treatment, a cure for it a thousand years go. But they didn't give a flying fuck. I got vitamin B shots from a doctor who was a friend of my husband, and that helped a bit. But that's about it. Other women would tell me that morning sickness was a sign of a healthy pregnancy, which was certainly a consolation. And I think that I endured it all with a genuine sense of martyrdom, determined to persevere, in the face of all the sexist, condescending bullshit, for the sake of my baby, for Mark's sake. And so, that first week in January of 1956, the third, on a Tuesday, my water broke. And Dr. Schneckendorf said come right into the hospital. I remember it was snowy and I had my little bag with me.

And Schneckendorf and all the residents told me, "What you need to do is walk. Walk up and down on the hall." So I walked up and down on the hall. I had my robe — a pale blue-and-white-printed corduroy robe with white linen embroidered collar and cuffs. Buttoned down the front. Like a college girl's. Slippers. Long, fair hair in a ponytail. And I'm walking, walking, walking...and the pain is getting a bit worse, but I'm thinking, *This actually isn't so bad, it's like bad cramps.* And this sallow-looking young man appears and he says, "Hello." I thought, *That's strange.* "What are you doing here?" he asked, in his very thick Italian accent. I thought that was obvious. "I'm in labor! What are *you* doing here?" "I'm an anesthesiologist," he replied. He was flirting with me! I thought that was the funniest thing. Imagine — making a pass at a pregnant woman in a maternity ward! I suppose men just think they can make use of their position whenever the whim strikes them, and women should think it's wonderful that they think you're sexy. "I love it, the green-eyed blondes," he said to me in his accent. Several hours later, I was screaming at the top of my lungs, and I knew what *real* labor was, what *real* pain was. And at three o'clock in the morning, after twelve hours of labor, with no painkillers until the very end, this nice, little, perfectly round head emerged. I was ecstatic at the sight of him. I was thrilled and happy and delighted. I was as overjoyed as a human being can be. From the moment I looked at him, I knew how wonderful he was and would always be. There was just this atavistic thrill. It was physical and emotional. My mother came to see us that morning, and she held him. And then the next day, when I woke up, I brushed my hair and brushed my teeth. And I looked up. And there was that young man again—the Italian anesthesiologist. And he had a bouquet of flowers! And again, this struck me as very, very amusing. Mario. His name was Mario. He was from a titled family in Italy, and he'd only been in the U.S. for a short period of time. It was the beginning of a funny friendship. He met Mark's father. He was a typical mad Italian driver. He had these Italian sports cars and got into frequent accidents. Mark's father, who had recently graduated from law school and was clerking for a judge at the time, would help this Mario with the legal ramifications of all his numerous car accidents. It was clear that he liked the way I looked and liked the way I spoke...that he thought I was a cut above the typical people he saw...When I look back, these aren't things I'm particularly fond of—that kind of class snobbery and being such a big flirt. Anyway, it was a week's stay in the hospital in those days—that was just the protocol then. And there I was, this thin, fragilelooking girl, but I was strong. I'd walk around and stand in front of the nursery window. And I could always immediately tell which cart he was in—those skinny, naked, red legs. They'd bring the baby every four hours to be fed, bottle-fed—I didn't nurse. His circumcision was scheduled for the last day that week—the *bris* with a *mohel*. And I was extremely anxious about that on every level. I'm very concerned about cleanliness. The idea of some old geezer with his own equipment filled me with foreboding. But I was reassured by Harry Gerner, the pediatrician, and by my parents and my in-laws. I had another issue, though. I have very serious problems with clotting. I have a genetic inability to clot properly and almost died getting my tonsils out when I was ten. I had massive hemorrhaging. So I demanded that before they even think of performing Mark's circumcision, they get a clotting time done. I insisted on it. And they did. And it was normal. And they had the bris, in a special room. I don't remember if I was wearing clothes or my robe. And all the grandparents were there. And it all went perfectly well. And the next day we went home. I can regale you with all the ensuing milestones—at ten days, he raised his head and rolled over; at six weeks, he giggled; at about five months he could crawl backwards, shake his head no, and play hide-and-seek; he stood up all alone and got his first teeth at six months; at six and a half months he stood up all alone holding on to the crib; he took his first steps holding on to his playpen at seven months; he said his first word, *Da-da,* at eight months, and walked all by himself at eleven months; his favorite toys were a set of colored disks on a chain and a stuffed fuzzy cocker spaniel that his uncle Richie gave him—because I dutifully recorded all of this critical information in a white satin–bound baby diary, in which I also inscribed the following account of his first birthday: "Mark had a birthday party on Sunday the 6th of January, and we took movies of him and all the family. Both Grandmas and Grandpas, Great-Grandmas and Great-Grandpas were there, and his aunts and uncles too. He received beautiful gifts, put both fists in the cake, cried at the company, and later in the evening 'performed' for them and for the camera."

By the following year, 1958, we'd moved to an apartment complex, a middle-income co-op, called College Towers, in the Greenville section of Jersey City. Mark was a toddler, two years old. And one afternoon, we were, uh, sitting outside in a sort of semicircular area of plantings out in front of our building. It was a new building and there were benches there, and it had to have been springtime or early summer because, for some silly reason, I even remember what I was wearing. I was sitting there with him, and I was in shirtsleeves. I had on the style of the day, for sportswear—sort of man-tailored stuff, you know, very preppy—you wore Bermuda shorts, and they didn't have a crease pressed in, they had a crease sort of stitched in, and khaki, and, um, loafers. I guess they were penny loafers. You put a dime in—I forget why. And a blue man-tailored shirt with the sleeves rolled up, a button-down, and that was sort of the style of the time for college girls and for, um, well-dressed young women. I was sitting there, long hair in a ponytail, feeling very happy and proud of him, my beautiful, wonderful, amazing boy, and happy with the weather and so on, and all of a sudden a little truck drove up, really small, and attached to the back of it was a slightly larger, uh, sort of little caboose thing, and on it was a small merry-go-round, a little gadget that just sort of went in a circle. And when I looked at it, the first thing I thought of was *Boy, that's an awfully small circle to be going around in.* There were other mothers out there, and other kids playing with each other, and they all heard...the little truck played a tune, I think. There was some way for everyone to know what it was, and what it was for...And the older children ran for it, and then the little kids like Mark. And the moms walked toward it, and people were getting on and paying, and he said to me, very clearly to me, that he wanted to get on, and I said, "Oh, okay, sweetie, we're going to do that right now." And the guy from the truck—the guy who operated the merry-go-round—said hello to me, and, um, I said hi back, and I was much more interested in putting Mark in safely. There were a couple of kids already on it. I put you in the little seat, and I was trying to figure out how to hook the little belt on you, and I see the guy go to sit in the front of the car and start something, and I started to say—whatever I said to him: "Uh, hey mister, sir, wait just a minute, just a minute or two please, I'm just putting him in," and he kept saying things like "That's okay, honey, that's okay, girlie, you can have a ride." And I kept saying, "No, you don't understand, no, I need to get off. This is my little boy. I'm just putting him on." And he started it. The music was starting, and he was still saying that—"All right honey, all right girlie." And all I could think of was that I was going to be dizzy and probably throw up. And one could say I talked myself into it, but the truth is I know my nature, and I knew I couldn't do that, and the circle was so small I knew nothing good was going to come out of that for me. And he thought—I don't know why I'm so sure of this, but I am—he thought that I was the babysitter. I was dressed like a teenager, and he thought I was a teenager, and what was I anyway—twenty-three years old, so...And I just kept saying to him, "Can you stop it now? And then you'll start it again." And he kept saying, "That's okay honey, that's all right girlie, you can, uh, it's all right, it's a free ride for you." And when it ended, and I took Mark off there, the world was still going round and round for me, and I was *so* nauseous and *so* dizzy. And he had had such a good time, and he did not want to go inside with me. He wanted to go on that ride again. But I had to take him inside, and I had to go lie down for a few minutes, because to that guy I might have been *girlie* and *honey* and it was okay, but it was pretty awful for me. So, that's the story of the merry-go-round. I usually think of myself as a very friendly, gregarious person, but thank the heavens, I never saw that man again. The people who lived directly below us—we were on the second floor of our building, they were on the first—were from somewhere in New York, and she had a very definite Brooklyn or Bronx accent, and they were not particularly educated people. They were working-class people, and I think she worked, and she became very friendly.

Um, I was...as I said, I tried to be friendly with everyone, but I wasn't looking to, y'know, have relationships
where I was obligated to spend time with other people. I felt very keenly my responsibility for my little boy,
and my desire was to spend as much time as possible
with him. But it was all very pleasant and cordial with
my neighbors, and there were no true problems, except
with this woman downstairs, who I thought was very
warm and loving and friendly to me, but who behaved
very badly. Mark was usually up very early in the morning. He was never a great sleeper, never ever, never ever.
And just when I thought I had it made—that we had
gotten past getting up during the night—he would get,
um, a runny nose or his schedule would be off, because
we went on a holiday or something, and we'd start sort
of all over again. He spoke very early, and he spoke very
clearly, and I would hear "Mommy," and it could be
the middle of the night, and I would come in and talk
to him and sometimes get him, and, um...This time in
particular that I'm thinking of, he had his first real cold,
and I know that he was then I guess either three and a
half or four because he went to the, uh, Jewish Community Center, to the nursery school, and that was the first
experience he had had with a real infection from the
other kids, 'cause otherwise he was pretty much pro-
tected from that kind of thing, and, to tell you the truth,
there were many times that I decided not to send him.
Either he wasn't better from a sniffle or Harry Gerner,
his pediatrician, whom I called Uncle Harry, and who

was my father's best friend, and who had also been *my* pediatrician, would say to me, "Must he go there?" Because Mark would almost invariably get ear infections after he had a cold. So, it was a very sort of divided-up experience. He didn't go regularly as I had expected him to, because of all these other things. But to get back to that dark-haired lady downstairs...when he did get better from whatever thing he'd had that interrupted his night's sleep, he clearly didn't want to go back to the habit of just hanging out in the crib or in the bed, and he would call me or he would come into the bedroom, and I would, I finally *had* to...Uncle Harry said, "You've got to put an end to this, you can't just keep getting up with him. You can't keep letting him know that he can do that to the two of you. You're the grown-ups." But the idea of letting him cry was not something I was happy with at all. But I would go in and...there were no books on the subject the way there are now, like the Ferber method, Ferbering, whatever it's called. I would come in, and I would talk to him, and I would say, "I'm not coming back now, I've been in here three times, I've been in here four times, it's the middle of the night—look outside, see, it's very dark out and your father is asleep, and everybody in the building is asleep, and I was asleep, and now I'm going to go back to sleep." And then sometimes I would come back in just one more time, and then finally I just realized I had to do it. And I let him cry. And he cried and he cried. And he called me and he called me and he cried. And it just made me heartbroken. But I knew that that one night was *the* night where I had to give it a try. And I would speak out to him every once in a while and say, "No, I'm not coming back, honey. In the morning, we'll talk, and in the morning, we'll go into the living room," etc. So she—the woman downstairs— called me the next day, and she let me have it. She said I was guilty of child abuse and she was going to call the police because I let my child scream all night. And she was right downstairs, and the sound could be heard. And it started the second night again, and then, about the middle of the night, he gave up. But she never forgave me, never forgave me for that, and that's when I realized that those kinds of casual friendships are just made, not because you really care about those people or you choose them because your interests are the same, but because you're sort of thrown together. And she was mostly a liar because she was not that worried about him, that's nonsense; she was worried about losing sleep, and she figured the way to not have that happen was to threaten me with something. Child abuse?! Can you imagine someone having the temerity to even insinuate such a thing? I simply adored Mark. There was nothing I wouldn't have done to make him happy and comfortable. I made sure that his crib was spotless and beautiful, that his bed was spotless and beautiful, that his room was lovely. I was fanatical about that. To a fault, actually. I had this carpet sweeper, and it had a mechanism inside that turns, that went around like this...and Mark must have either moved his hand at that moment or I was just being clumsy and an idiot for having it out...Why did I have to carpet-sweep while he was playing there, why? Something must have just broken or spilled or a box of crackers fell down or something of that sort and of course being me, I just was going to get rid of it right away, and all of a sudden his little hand was there and I rode over one of his fingers and caught it there. It was caught in there. I remember that trying to get it out was horrific, and he was screaming in pain, and it might have even been his whole little hand that was caught in there. But one finger was looking very damaged and purple. And I ran with him into the bathroom, and I know that what I did to him hurt like anything, but I put it under the cold water, and I kept rubbing it and trying to keep it straight and trying to see if there was a broken bone or anything in it. And I felt like I was doing that for hours while he was screaming, but it actually couldn't have been for more than a few minutes. And then I dried it off and patted it, and he was still very, uh...he was still in great pain. He was in *real* pain. I don't remember going to the doctor. I remember calling Uncle Harry, Harry Gerner. He asked some questions about whether Mark could move his fingers, and I made him, once we could get the pain under some control, uh, I made him move his fingers then, because if anything had been broken...I don't know what they do about something like that anyway, whether they set it or what...Ugh!

Ugh! How horrible! I still think about it! Anyway, as I mentioned before, Mark was never a great sleeper and typically he'd be up by five thirty or six in the morning, and, uh, we would have breakfast and talk to each other, and he'd look at his books and, depending on the age, sometimes I would read to him, and then a little later, when he really memorized, he would look at them himself and he would read some of them back to me. And we would talk about what we were going to do during the day, and if it was a bad day or wintertime or rain or whatever, we would decide whether we were going to stay in or go out or, um, if we were going to, in fact, walk over to Nana Harriet's or go to the supermarket which was right near there, or go out to play in front of the building where there would be other kids, or the myriad other things that would be on the agenda. Sometimes his father would come and pick us up and bring us to Nana Rose's house, but mostly the days went along with just the two of us... And it was a delightful, heavenly time for us. Until my second pregnancy. The period during which I was pregnant with my second baby was a very difficult time for me. It was a very difficult pregnancy with a very tragic outcome. I was feeling really terribly ill most of the time and I tried to not let Mark know. He was still a very little boy. And I don't really even know how much he was aware of then, because I never really asked him in the years following that. I didn't want to bring it up again—first of all, it was still painful to me, because we didn't have a baby to bring home and, um, I didn't want to discuss that time over and over again. I felt guilty because, for a number of months during the pregnancy, I had to have him in the care of my mother, and I just was so ill...My doctor this time wasn't Schneckendorf, the doctor who'd delivered Mark, it was a different man, it was this guy who was very popular with all the young mothers...I don't remember his name maybe because I don't want to. He had a reputation for keeping people well sedated so there was no pain, or as little as possible, and I thought, well, I could use that because I was in labor for so long with Mark that I thought, well, that's sort of dumb of me to, you know, to go looking for that kind of thing again, this would be much better. And then, um, feel good, feel strong, blah-blah-blah. Well nobody knows about these things and how they're going to happen, but it turns out that this man did every single thing that he could...put it in another way—everything he did was the wrong thing. When I was throwing up constantly and I couldn't hold anything down in the very beginning of that pregnancy, he clapped me in the hospital. Because he thought he was going to snap me out of this thing. I think he was obviously a misogynist, and he obviously thought this was like a spoiled-girl reaction to being pregnant. You know? That, uh, if I had more to do...that's what many men said about this, y'know, if you had more to think about...So he clapped me in the hospital and gave me something called Thorazine, which gave me a reaction that was written about in the *New England Journal of Medicine.* I couldn't stop my arms from shaking, my voice was *way up like this,* and I couldn't stay still. I clawed at the sheets, and I was miserable, and I couldn't rest, and I was hyper, and I said, "Get me out of here." I said, "This is not helping. What is this about? There's nothing wrong with my mind. I'm not emotionally ill. I'm nauseous from being pregnant. Get me out of here, this is awful." And I said to Mark's father, "If you don't take me out today, I am gonna crawl out on my hands and knees." I was all bloody down both arms, with scabs from doing this, from clawing on the rough hospital linens. And I said, "Just get me out of here. Without the doctor's permission, just sign me out! Take me home!" And, one way or another, I was finally released. And I was profoundly grateful to be home after that, and everything was fine then—until the hemorrhage. I bent down one night to tie Mark's shoe—we were at my mom's and we were just about ready to go home, we'd had dinner there, and I was in, oh, I guess my third month—and as I bent down to tie his shoe, I started to hemorrhage. And I had to go back to the hospital. And I was there a couple of days, at that horrible place where they did nothing positive for me at all, back at that hospital for a couple of days, until they felt that was under control. And then this doctor said that to me, "There is nothing wrong. The heartbeat is very strong. You're a nice strong girl. Everything is perfect." And I said, "But I bled buckets. How is that okay?"

And he said, "Well..."—he said this prophetically—
"well, sometimes the fetus isn't as firmly attached to
the uterus as it should be, and that's why you hemor-
rhaged, but everything is fine now, it's fine." And, um,
then, when I got home this time, I was told I had to
stay in bed for at least a month—a stupid idea under
any circumstances, but particularly stupid under those
circumstances, because if I had gotten up...I should
have run up and down about four thousand stairs, because if I had had a miscarriage, it would have been the
best thing that could have happened. Instead, during
that time, I didn't even understand what was happening to me. I tried to stay still and sleep as much as
possible and not be as nauseous and as miserable as I
was, and Mark would come in and I'd talk to him and
he'd talk to me. And he was pretty happy with Nana
Harriet while the two of us were at her house, living
there for that month, but I knew he wanted more from
me...I knew that...and I felt terribly guilt-ridden. I
never got over feeling that I had ruined his life, that I
had done something terrible to him by showing my own
weakness in that way and not being there for him. Nev-
ertheless, it didn't act out in that way. Right after we
came home, I seemed to feel a lot better, certainly never
really good, but enough better so I could take care of
him. I was very nauseous through the entire pregnancy.
I was extremely nauseous all the time with each of my
pregnancies, but this was worse because I was much
weaker. But Mark and I would talk and play, and I was

so grateful to be home and to be with him, and he was so wonderful to talk to, and we would sing together. He's the only person (along with his sister, Chase) who has ever heard me sing, and it's lucky for the rest of the world that they haven't, but the two of them seemed to like it. And we would play games and I would say, "Would you like to walk over to Grandma's now, wanna go see Nana?" And, um, he didn't know that he was actually walking me. He would hold my hand and we would talk to each other and he—I was his security, which I was supposed to be, but he was mine too. And he was such, always, always, such an interesting person to talk to, and we would really talk to each other, and I never understood quite the women who were so angry at having to be home with their kids, angry that they had no one to talk to and their interests were, um, pitiful because all they could do is talk baby talk to babies. And our life was nothing like that. I didn't talk baby talk to him and he didn't talk baby talk back to me. He had questions about things, I had stories to tell him, and he had stories to tell me, and I honestly and absolutely loved our time together and never ever felt as if I was missing something that would have been better than that. So the rest of that pregnancy was "fine"— I just didn't tell anyone that I threw up every single day, several times a day, and, um, this doctor kept saying things to me like "Look at your hands. Look how beautiful your hands are! What a lovely-looking girl you are." And, um, "What a beautiful child you have. And this child will be a beautiful child." And stuff like that. But that wasn't the answer to any of the questions I really had. I knew that. But I couldn't have possibly known how badly this was going to end. I went into labor and I went to the hospital and I was knocked for a loop by this doctor. And next thing I knew...well, the next thing I knew was nothing—I was fast asleep, I was out of it. The truth is, what he should have done is, the moment I called him or the day or so before that, he should have been seeing me virtually every day then, in the ninth month, and he should have taken me into the hospital, and either done a cesarean or induced labor and watched me every moment. Because while I was out of it, the placenta—that's what the fetus is attached to, the placenta—the placenta, which was clearly weak to begin with, burst. And from what I've been told years since, I'm lucky I didn't die. Or needed an immediate hysterectomy at that moment. And the baby was without oxygen—beautiful, beautiful little girl, beautiful dark-haired, perfect-looking little girl...Not a chance, because he was an incompetent. And that guy I told you about, the Italian anesthesiologist, he happened to be in the hospital that day, and he told us later, he might have told your father earlier on, but he told me when he thought I could handle talking about it that he was there and that this man was completely incompetent in the face of what was happening. And so after the birth when I woke up, there were two people punching me in the belly, kneading me, pushing,

pushing, pushing, pushing, pushing. Because they had to get everything, every piece, every tiny little piece out, otherwise you can die of fever. So in those senses, I was very lucky, I suppose...But they kept me there a week, which is what they did in those days. Instead of just keeping me overnight or a day or so, and then letting me out of there, away from the sounds of crying infants and the sight of crying infants and happy infants, they made me stay and they thought they were doing something wonderful for me...it was simply the protocol of the day. And the woman they put me in the room with, thinking they were being very compassionate, this woman had a baby who had, um, hemophilia, so that baby was not brought into the room, that baby was having special care in the nursery until about the fourth day, when they felt he was strong enough to come to her. And that's when I said to Mark's father to tell the people at the hospital either you release me or I am getting dressed and I am going home. This is beyond bearing. It's a useless terrible thing that you're doing. And all right...all kinds of hormones are still very active and, uh, I was not made to feel better, by the way, by the people who kept telling me how lucky I was. That doesn't work. If anyone wants to know how to help somebody who's having something awful happening to them, you don't tell them they're lucky because they have a beautiful wonderful child and a great family and a husband who adores you and how beautiful you were and um, what a great life you had and how young you were. And I couldn't stop the tears, I was sobbing, but they just kept running out of my eyes and I couldn't stop the wetness, it just kept happening. And I knew I had to get out of there and that it was not good. I needed to be able to be just with the people whom I cared about, who cared about me, and I needed to start to live some kind of normal life, and I needed to get away from this a little bit, and not be pushed in this way. There were also a couple of other awful things that happened, or one at least. The head nurse, the day that I was leaving, clearly didn't like us, didn't like the looks of my husband, of my father, and didn't like the way I looked. Uh, to her we were just rich Jews, and she really had such hatred, and it was made very clear, because the day I was getting dressed to leave and I was waiting for Joel to pick me up, she came in and she said, "There's a question I have to ask you because the proper protocol has not been followed, and I don't know what to do because I'm having a problem." And I said, "Why don't you just wait. I don't want to talk about anything that's going on. Please wait for my husband and my father. They'll be here in a little while. If you have papers to fill out or questions to ask, please ask them." And she said, "But this is absolutely urgent. We have to know what to do with the baby's body." She couldn't wait to come in to me to talk about my dead baby's body. Out of spite. Oh, yes. When I turned to look at her, I could not even really believe what I was hearing. She had such a look of sort of satisfaction on her face, to be able to approach me with something that was going to make me feel terrible. I think this was both a class thing and an anti-Semitic thing, but I could be wrong about one or the other. It was very definitely a socioeconomic thing. She didn't like the way we spoke, she didn't like the way we looked or dressed. It was all much too much for her. I assumed that she knew we were Jews, and that my father and indeed Mark's father looked Jewish—I don't know about me, it's hard to tell about yourself…I just could not wait to get out of there. I walked toward her, as I remember, one or two steps, because I really wanted to just do something horrible to her, but I was mostly…I was too weak at that point emotionally, I showed my feelings, the tears just rolled down my face, so I couldn't act tough because I just wasn't quite ready for that. I could have said awful things to her and I said whatever I said, like "That is a horrible thing to say to me, and I told you that I'm not speaking to you about any of these things. Get out of the room now. I'm getting dressed to go home." And the truth is, and I've lived to rue this, that I never knew what they did with my little girl. And I would have liked to know where she went, and I would have liked some kind of dignity, to the poor little creature who didn't have a chance to have a life.

Mark was with one or both of his grandparents and, uh, it was pretty gruesome for me until I finally came home. And when I did get home, he said to me either that day or the next day, he said, "Mommy, you made a promise and you didn't keep your promise." And I said, "What do you mean, honey?" And he said, "You told me that you were going away for a couple of days to the hospital and you were going to bring home our baby. Where is our baby?" So that was very hard, that kind of thing, because I tried to be perfectly calm and explain that that wasn't going to happen this time, but that sometime soon we would talk about it and think about it, and maybe we would be able to get a baby for him to play with. Um, after that the family situation was...my mother only wanted to know that I was all right, and that Mark was all right, and that our little family was all right. And she did not want to see me being sad. I mean, she knew. She was a woman, and she knew about this. She didn't have to see me being sad. She knew. But my father, a guy, he didn't want to know, and he wouldn't know, and by saying everything was fine, and by saying, You're fine, you're absolutely fine, everything in your life is fine, everything is wonderful, you're here, it's good...And in the face of that kind of thing, I simply had to act like I was fine. By the next summer, when I was away with everybody at the shore, my behavior...I can look back now and see that I was irrational some of the time. My temper was out of control. It was very hard living with Francis, my sister. And the kids...if they did anything to Mark...Adam, my nephew, was a biter. I flew off the handle. I couldn't take very well the happiness of other people with their babies, or even if they weren't happy with them, the fact that other people had babies who were born the same time. I was not behaving well, I just wasn't...I guess I deserved a bit of a pass for some of that, because I don't remember ever being able to sit down with anyone, and that included Mark's father, and really discuss the depths of my pain at that point. And a special kind of pain and anger that came along with it because I blamed myself. I blamed my body, and it was almost as if a malignant fate, a malign fate was punishing me...punishing me for having spent a whole lifetime being proud of my body because it was beautiful. It's not that I thought I'd actually done anything wrong, except that it was like an ugly slap in the face, because my body betrayed me, at least that's the way I interpreted it some of the time. So that summer, I was really acting out, I know I was...I remember I slapped my aunt Beatrice across the face. That's the thing I remember the most that shows how completely wacko I was. She was an overbearing person and bossy, and she said something to me that I didn't take well, and instead of just telling her to mind her own business or whatever, I just reached over and gave her a good one across the face. And nobody was going to get back at me either, so I really was able to act out...But how many months later was that? Uh, half a year or so...so I guess the worst of it was over by the time I got home from the shore and, uh, we resumed our everyday life pretty much. And Mark kept me sane, because being together, and I don't mean...this must sound...If anybody else outside of the family heard this, they would think that I was being a creepy mother, like climbing all over him, but it wasn't like that at all. It was just good. It was just happy and, um, profoundly wonderful, especially in the face of so many other kids I could see outside and their behavior. Mark was smart. He was interesting. His reaction to some of the things that kids did was very, very funny to me and very cute. He was an observer of things. Where some kids just would come, they would see a big pile of kids falling all over each other and digging, or getting in the mud, and he'd go over and he was interested—very! And he would go over reasonably quickly, but he would look at it all first and then make a decision about if it was something he really wanted to dive into or whether he would think, *This is* stupid, *I'm not gonna do this!* And then he would back up a little and wait for some of them to come muddied out of there. So it was good, so good for me to have him, but the next couple of years a part of me always felt unfinished, that I had something I had to do that I really needed to do. I didn't think he was consciously aware of what had happened. He did not seem interested to find out any of the details, he never ever said anything to me about, Mommy where were you, why were you lying in bed in Grandma's house? And I thought I had damaged him so deeply psychologically that he was not going to come up with this until he was grown, and then he would blame me for all of these things. But that never happened, that never happened...But, look, I'm sure that seeing me lie there like that couldn't have been a happy experience for him. I must have looked like a zombie. I must have weighed practically nothing. And the rest of the time, I did not sit about crying, and I didn't walk around with a mad face, and I didn't fight with his father, but I used to wait until about two in the morning, and then I would cry quietly and think about the fact that my sister-in-law had a baby, and my sister had a baby, all born, all born at the same time, and I think Barbara Kass and a whole bunch of other people, the Ginigers, the people from the art gallery in New York...And just I didn't. And so we tried to adopt a child about a year and a half later or a year and three-quarters later. Some friend, no, some relative of my mom's friend...what was her name? Um, I'm not gonna remember, uh...Dora...Dora Tanner...Dora Tanner had a sister and brother-in-law in Trenton. He was a pharmacist, and somehow, I guess through my dad, the pharmacist called my father and said that one of his customers was a young woman who already had, like, one or two illegitimate children, and Catholic Charities was helping her, and this guy was an Italian boy who worked in a gas station. She was a Polish girl and, um, she was pregnant again, and she didn't want to keep the child, and she asked him whether anyone in his family wanted to adopt the baby, and, to make a long story short...I don't remember any of the details...My dad and Joel did all the legal and proper things that you're allowed to do. You're not allowed to give somebody extra money or buy a baby, but you are allowed to help with the care and the pregnancy and stuff, you know. So, then I washed all the baby clothes again, and scrubbed and polished the crib and set it up in your room and we talked about having a baby and, uh, I didn't make too much out of it, but there was talk about it and I was actively setting up a space, and I drove to Trenton with Joel and Grandpa Ray, and they went in to pick up the baby, and Catholic Charities had come and taken it away, and said she would be, uh, um, I just lost the word...um, what they did to Spinoza? Um...she would be *excommunicated*. She wouldn't get any more money from the Catholic Charity, and they would see to it that she lost her other children, whatever it was they said. And there I was again coming home...It was a little boy, it would have had the best life any little boy ever had. I was scared to be pregnant again. I was scared that maybe something was wrong with me, and that I would kill another baby, and then I finally had to get a grip on myself. And I said to myself, *All right, okay, you're twenty-five, twenty-six years old, grow up! This is what you're going to have to do. You want a baby, you're gonna have to have another baby, you're going to be nauseous every single day, and if you have to keep that to yourself and not tell any of these morons, these men who are doctors, you won't tell them, but you're going to do this and get through it and you're going to take one more shot at this.* And I got pregnant immediately. And I threw up every day several times. But it was the best pregnancy I had because I knew what was ahead of me every day, and I'll be damned if I was

gonna let it beat me another time. *Not!* And Mark was
in school, James F. Murray No. 38 Elementary School.
We had moved to a little house on Westminster Lane,
right off the Boulevard. And he was five and a half,
and he would answer the phone and he would say, "My
mommy's busy vomiting, but she'll call you back later."
And I would bring him to school and pick him up.
But there was one symbol, one experience that showed
me that he had...that he was very conscious of having been abandoned by me before. Nana Harriet was
supposed to pick him up from school one day, and she
came to the wrong door, or came at the wrong time,
and missed him. And from then on for the next number
of months, I had to stand outside, and Mrs. Brown, I
think her name was, Mrs. Brown would hold him up—
he was so adorable anyway, and all the teachers fell
in love with him; it was very unfair, because they just
wanted him right in front of them—this Mrs. Brown
would hold him up to the window so he could see his
mommy standing out in the street like an idiot, and I
would wave at him until that came to an end, whenever,
after however many weeks or months I had to do that.
And that was a symbol to me that that was...like, we're
talking about an overreaction to just that one thing, and
that it stood for all of the other things that he really did
remember, that he really did. But this pregnancy with
Mark's sister, Chase, was not horrible in the sense that
I wasn't taken away anywhere. I used a practice that
was a very well known, conservative Catholic practice.

Dr. Cosgrove Sr. was like, he was the boss of the world. He used to call all the women "girlie," but these two guys, Dr. Dolan and Dr. Cosgrove Jr., treated me very well, and treated me like I was a normal person and everything was fine, and they were kind and funny and they said to me, You have nothing to worry about, and if there was anything to worry about we would be there every minute, and we would take you to wherever you had to go, if it was a different hospital, and you have nothing to worry about, nothing. The truth is the two of them were scared out of their minds. I was probably the only patient they ever had who... This was a big rich practice. The two of them were at Chase's delivery, the two of them, the whole labor, they were there. They didn't move from there. They had resident pediatricians, they had blood people, hematologists. That was the most crowded delivery room you ever saw. And, uh, that was a very happy day for all of us, and I brought her home, and Mark was so thrilled. He was just so delighted with her. She was the best baby. She slept a lot and she was very cute, and finally one day he came home from school, and I used to have to—not *have* to, I used to *try* to—arrange her naps so that I wasn't taking time away from just our time together, Mark's and my time. But he finally said to me, "Mommy? Don't you like our baby? You really love our baby, don't you? You like to be with her, right?" And I said, "Well, sure honey. Why would you ask such a thing?" And he said, "Because she's always sleeping." But then everything was very natural really, from then on. She was very good, Mark was very, very good with her. The age difference was such that...I have a picture of him giving his two index fingers to her when she started to walk, she was about, what, ten or eleven months old, and he was helping her walk through the living room. Because he was a big boy...and he had friends and a dog...It was a very, very happy time for me, and my pride, and I hope it's not *just* pride, I hope it was the truth—that I did not, as much as it was humanly possible for me, let him be really affected by the other things. There were times of course when I was taken away or when my expression might have revealed my feelings, even if I tried not to show it. But for the most part, he had an extremely happy babyhood and childhood, and, um, the worries I had about him were about his ear infections, and when we moved away, I was very concerned with him in the new school and whether it would be all right, and those are the things that every parent thinks about. He started to get earaches. Um, he would get a cold, or uh...I don't know whether it would be a sinus infection or just a regular cold, but children's ears aren't on an angle like adults'. The tube in the ear on adults is on an angle so that it drains out, and with small children it goes straight across, so the infected material lies in there and becomes...the material lies in there and then becomes infected and that's very painful, very painful. And he would get them frequently, practically whenever he got a cold, as a secondary infection. And this led to him getting his tonsils out, yes, because that's what they did—adenoids and tonsils. And that was a serious mistake that I made, and I get bad marks for that one. I made him a promise. First of all, we took him to New York. It was horrible. We took him to Columbia Presbyterian because I was being elitist about where to go, and because I had had, as a child, a horrific experience in Jersey City, so there was no way I was staying around there. But I promised him...he asked me if I was going to be there when he woke up and be with him, and I said yes, and they wouldn't let me upstairs, and instead of tearing that hospital limb from limb, and screaming and carrying on like a banshee and saying, "I'm going to get my child now! That's my child, not yours, mine!" which I'm perfectly capable of doing now. Why did I sit there like that? He didn't talk to me for about two or three days afterward. He wouldn't talk to me. I'd lied. I told him something, and he woke up in pain, and I wasn't there. So, I'm a jerk. I did what the adults assumed I would do because I have to do it, and I should not have done that. I should have gone upstairs and grabbed him and been with him. Because I'd promised I would be there with him when he woke up, and because he needed me. And they were wrong, and that would have been right. So I've made more than my share of mistakes I'll tell you that. Ugh!

By the way, I have pictures, if anyone would like to see them after the reading, pictures from the years in between. Pictures of Mark and I playing shuffleboard in Deal, of him and his father and me going to New England, going to the Cape... That was the summer after I lost the baby and you could sort of tell looking at me, how skinny I was, you know, that I was still sad. Would you guys like to see the pictures?

PANDA EXPRESS WORKER
(Scrolling through his Instagram.)

Huh?

MARK'S MOTHER

Would you guys like to see the pictures of how skinny I was and still sad?

PANDA EXPRESS WORKER

No, that's all right.

MARK'S MOTHER

Well, looking out at this food court tonight, I can't help but think about how intermixed books and food have always been for Mark. Books were mixed with everything that we did and some of that was purposeful, because I went to stores with him and without him and bought him books, so that was, of course, uh, a thought-out thing. Books were very important in my life and in my house growing up, and it would never have occurred to me to raise him without a lot of books around, but it was clear very early on that books were very important to him. So we had mutual interests even when he was a year and a half or a year old. And he named some of his books. They were "eating books." He was a slow eater, and, um, I don't know whether he consciously was concerned about whether he had an appetite enough to really eat a good dinner or a good lunch or whether he just felt he would enjoy it more, which is more likely, if he had those particular books, *The Tawny Scrawny Lion* or *The Musicians of Bremen,* in front of him. And, uh, those were wonderful, funny days, and there were also other funny things about it that I'm sure he doesn't know. We didn't have any real money; his father was just about beginning his practice, and when Mark was born, Joel had been clerking for a judge, and you make virtually nothing. So when I would get lamb chops, from my mother's kosher butcher, or wherever else I got them, I would cook them for Mark, I would get them and give them to him for lunch and for his dinner. It wasn't what his father and I were having for dinner, and he would get the meat. I would cut...like if it was two or three little rib chops, I would cut up all the meat, and that was for him, and I would be salivating, and I would eat the bone when we were finished. And sometimes he would nibble on a bone, but he didn't seem to care about that as much as I did. I should have known from those days that he was the person who was going to like rare meat. But I liked the crispy well-done part, and I couldn't wait to get hold of those bones and eat them, but I was…When I was growing up, and I could see from the way that my mother behaved, that everything was for the children, I mean, that's simply the way it was, and without consciously making a decision that the *kinder* or the children were the important thing, that was certainly the case. Everything was done to make him comfortable and clean and some of that was for my own ego I'm sure. I liked the way it looked, I liked the way he looked, I liked the way it appeared to me that I was capable, you know…as I said, his crib was beautiful and his room was lovely, and everything that he had was crisp and at the same time soft, and he never ever had dirty, torn play clothes, it just wasn't like that. But it also turned out that he was a pretty clean kid and a pretty clean-lookin' kid. And he was very easy to take places. He sat there quietly, I mean, he didn't have temper tantrums and carry on like his sister, Chase. I used to have to carry Chase out of places under my arm. But Mark and I would go to the office in Journal Square, take the bus sometimes, and go up to the office and have lunch downstairs with his grandpa Ray or with his father and with his uncle Lewis. And we'd have lunch at the Bird Cage at Lord & Taylor's—that's when we

moved to the suburbs and I had a car, so it was a little easier, and we would just go to the Bird Cage. And
I know Mark loved it there. I was always very careful
and very caring about the food he ate. When Mark was
an infant, Harry Gerner wouldn't let me feed him regular food the way, for example, Phyllis Leyner did. She
stuffed huge globs full of food into those kids' mouths,
like they were grown-ups, and Rose couldn't bear it.
And Uncle Harry said, No, one food at a time, and
when we know his reaction to that, 'cause his father
is very allergic and you know we've got to watch out
for those things, and that's the way I do it. So the first
thing he had was rice cereal, he liked it a lot, and then,
like, two weeks or three weeks, whatever, he had applesauce, same thing, same thing, then after that I think it
was some other fruit, I don't remember exactly...pears
was one of them. But I don't remember the others. But
then finally when we got to meat and vegetables and
that stuff, I knew the drill, but he was eating the ground
chicken and potatoes and sweet potatoes and carrots—
carrots he loved and sweet potatoes he loved. I remember that the applesauce he loved, but by that time the
rice cereal was okay, but it certainly wasn't a big treat.
That was the first regular food, so then it seemed like
a big deal, but months later he knew the other things
seemed more interesting. But then it was time to start
some of the more esoteric vegetables, so I bought beets
and green beans or whatever, and I had the little tiny
baby spoon, which is really little! And I just dipped the

end of it into the beets, so I had about *that* much on a spoon that was about *that* big, and just the little edge over there was beets, and I put it in his beautiful little pink mouth and he sort of—his eyes got very round and he sort of rolled it around for a couple of seconds and then he went *spew!*...I had beets in my eyelashes. I had beets up my nose. I had beets on my clothes. You would have thought that I had given him a quart of beets! And I thought, *That does it, he'll never get*...I rolled it around, it was on him, it was on his clothing, it was on the table. And I don't think I gave him beets again until he was pretty grown up. He likes beets now. Well, it just shows you.

Ladies and gentlemen, I give you Mark Leyner.

PART II

READING

MARK

Before I start, I'd like to say: Fuck everyone who said I was too paradoxical a hybrid of arrogant narcissism and vulnerable naïveté to succeed in life (even though they were right). Also, I'd like to dedicate this to all the nematodes and hyperthermophilic bacteria who live in deep-water sulfide chimneys around the world. Good days are coming, boys.

My mom gave me a ride here tonight, and, uh... I don't really like to talk to her when she's been drinking and she's driving over ninety miles an hour, because I don't want to distract her, so I was just sitting there in the passenger seat, looking out the window, sort of *musing* to myself... I think that mothers and sons, silent in a car, sometimes exchange telepathic soliloquies, but perhaps because we sensed that this could be our last night

together, that one or both of us might very well be assassinated tonight, we left each other to our respective
musing...that whole implosion of semioticity that is *musing,* that hypercaffeinated chatter of anthropomorphic
cartoon animals in one's head that is *musing,* that whole
danse macabre of singing little piglets in one's head...At
ninety miles per hour, the empirical world rushes past
in an impressionistic blur. You're thinking, *There's some
weird, retro-looking, brown transgendered individual jerking off in
the woods.* And then you're like, *No, that's a tree.* But sitting
there—the eternal little man, inflated with dreams of
flamboyant success but forced back on his own futility—
my memories of childhood were not impressionistic at
all, they were hyperrealistic. My mind's eye—my mind's
eyeball—had shot back, it had shot back to 1961...and
I, uh...I could see myself at the age of five, I could see
myself there so vividly...I was a little boy, playing on a
hot concrete alley on Westminster Lane in Jersey City
one day...God spoke to this little boy, as He speaks to
all pure-hearted children, in his simple, binary language
of blue sky and radiant sun. And suddenly, in a kind of
seizure, in an explosion of unfurling clairvoyance, he saw
everything that would ensue in his life. *Everything.* His
entire autobiography fast-forwarded in the most extra-
ordinary detail. The birth of his daughter, his prostate
cancer, his books (every word of them!), these final moments in this food court, in this mall, tonight. *Everything.*
So we have two of the mind's eyeballs, the mind's eyeball
of a fifty-eight-year-old man seated in the passenger seat

of his mother's car, daydreaming as he stares out the window and the mind's eyeball of a drooling five-year-old boy with blond bangs seated rigidly on a concrete alley, one speeding back in time from 2014, one speeding into the future from 1961. Assuming they are traveling at approximately the same warp speed, they would collide at around 1988, the year Pan Am Flight 103 exploded over Lockerbie, Scotland, and an earthquake in Armenia killed sixty thousand people. These are the uncanny transtemporal ballistics of the mind's eyeballs. And this is one of the things we (my mother and I) mean by *Gone with the Mind*.

Okay…just a little background before I get started: *Gone with the Mind* was originally going to be an autobiography in the form of a first-person shooter / flight-simulator game. And it was going to start at a breakfast meeting with my old editor Michael Pietsch during which I'm either assassinated or "commit suicide" in the men's room. And my ghost has to travel back in time, revisit each transformative event in my life, and execute or otherwise degrade or disable the central dramatis personae in order to get to the next (prior) event. The, uh…the *goal* of the game is to successfully reach my mother's womb, in which I attempt to unravel or unzip my father's and mother's DNA in the zygote, which will free me of having to eternally repeat this life. And I'm ferried from event to event by Benito Mussolini, who pilots a flying balcony. And along the way, he offers counsel and gaming advice kind of like Krishna in the Bhagavad Gita or like Virgil in Dante's *Inferno*. And if the player succeeds in unknitting the entirety of his (my) life, thus flinging himself into utter oblivion, into an ontological black hole (or to put a more positive spin on it, reintegrating himself into the oceanic void), he wins.

I think an autobiography in the form of a first-person shooter game that ends with unraveling the zygote in your mother's uterus *sounds* really cool, and Michael and pretty much everyone I mentioned it to also thought it *sounded* really cool, but what *is* that, actually? I mean, what would a book like that actually be, y'know? Once you start thinking about sitting down and actually writing something, it's an entirely different matter. But I remained totally committed to doing it, because that's just the kind of person I am—I'm not going to bail on something I said I was going to do. I think I'm a sort of exceedingly boring person (which certainly doesn't make me the best candidate for an autobiography!)...I mean *boring* in that I'm very dutiful, very responsible...and if I say I'm going to write an autobiography in the form of a first-person shooter game that ends with unraveling the zygote in your mother's uterus then I'm going to write an autobiography in the form of a first-person shooter game that ends with unraveling the zygote in your mother's uterus, and that's that. And I expect that of other people too, by the way. If you say you're going to be in the schoolyard waiting for me in a certain place at a certain time, then be at that place at that time. Don't send some proxy who doesn't even know where the hell to wait, y'know what I mean? If you say you're going to stay overnight with me at the hospital when I get my tonsils out, then stay overnight at the hospital, for God's sake.

I said I'm an exceedingly boring person...I don't *really* think that. I think I'm a sort of weird composite of thrill-seeking heedlessness and crippling hyperanxiety— I mean, I've taken LSD before a root canal, but I'm equally capable of calling the police and area hospitals if my wife is even five minutes late coming home from a pedicure, so...

At some point in this preliminary stage when I'm still just trying to figure out what this book could actually be, the Imaginary Intern appears...which changes *everything*. I was sitting on the toilet one morning, gazing down at the tiles on the bathroom floor, uh...just staring at the vein patterns and at the craquelure on this one particular tile, and I discerned a legible face...I discerned the lineaments of the Imaginary Intern in the craquelure of a tile on the bathroom floor. That's exactly how the Imaginary Intern was conjured up. This is a textbook *delusion of reference,* specifically a *pareidolia,* a psychological phenomenon that involves seeing meaningful patterns, frequently faces, in random information— a common example of which is, um...something like seeing the face of Jesus in a Cool Ranch Dorito or something along those lines.

The Imaginary Intern initially functioned mainly as a kind of archivist or production manager on *Gone with the Mind,* helping me collate and categorize autobiographical material, but soon he became more like a, I don't know...more like a coach or a trainer. Y'know that term in pharmacology, *mechanism of action?* It's the specific biochemical interaction that basically enables a drug to do what it does. When you're writing something, its mechanism of action is a very difficult thing to identify. It's a very subtle, very elusive thing. But it really is *the* crucial fucking thing. And when I felt that I'd lost it, that I suddenly just didn't know what it was...or when, y'know, I just felt kind of discouraged or dispirited about how it was all going, the Imaginary Intern would exhort me, he'd pump me up, y'know? He'd be, like, "Denzel Washington can land a plane upside down stinking drunk, and you can't write an autobiography? A book about your own life? Are you *fucking* kidding me?"

So, quickly on, he became a very active collaborator with me, very much a creative partner, and the fundamental principles of the project, its...what's that word?...its...its *donnée,* began to evolve quite rapidly.

I'm trying to think of a good way to describe the Imaginary Intern...um...He sort of reminded me of Billy Name, the guy who designed Andy Warhol's Silver Factory on East Forty-Seventh Street back in the early sixties, the guy who pretty much functioned as the Factory's foreman during its most fecund years...He was

very earnest and forthright and affirmative in a sort of
Jeff Koons / Ferris Bueller way...I'm not sure if any
of this is really helping give you a sense of what the
Imaginary Intern was actually like (and I'm going to talk
more about him—and especially about when he left,
which was a pretty big, traumatic deal for me—in a few
minutes), but, for now...I mean...he was just a very
friendly, very smart, upbeat, hardworking guy. Youth-
ful, eager, open-minded, pragmatic...very much in sync
with what I was thinking (obviously!) and very adept at
devising practical solutions to notions that were fanciful
or completely hypothetical. I was always struck by his
antipathy for abstraction and how constantly he was on
the alert for whatever smacks of mere theory as against
the solidity and efficacy of worldly practice.

I'd wash a Klonopin down with a beer and sit on
the couch and mute the TV, and I'd picture the Imaginary Intern and me just strolling down a long Brutalist
concrete promenade leading to an abyss, walking and
talking...

The Imaginary Intern could get very enthusiastic,
very excited by our ideas, very animated, sometimes
even a little strident, whereas I'd tend, as the night progressed, to become more and more recessive and sedate,
and I'd sort of tilt my head and purse my lips and just
listen. And I know sometimes that sort of bugged the
Imaginary Intern. And one morning, after I woke up, I
came downstairs and there was a note left on the couch
in the Imaginary Intern's handwriting:

Yes, it was late,
and, yes, I was being very
dented-in-the-head-mutant-hillbilly,

But you . . .
you just sat there
like some shitty poem.

And I remember thinking, *That's such a lovely line—*
"you just sat there / like some shitty poem."

Once I said to the Imaginary Intern that reading about
Achilles defiling the corpse of Hector gave me a hard-
on. Do you think that makes me a fascist? I asked him.
And he paused for what seemed like an eternity, and finally asked me if I knew that German soldiers on the
front called crystal meth *Panzerschokolade* (which means
"tank chocolate"), and we talked about how the world
could be divided between people with *sitzfleisch* and people with *shpilkes,* and about how movies of a certain era
used the donning of a frilly apron to signify how effete or
inadequate a man was (for example, Jim Backus in *Rebel
Without a Cause* or James Stewart in *The Man Who Shot
Liberty Valance*), and about how the government not only
knows that there's life after death, they know that life after death is fantastic, and they're suppressing it, because
they don't want everyone finding out and immediately
committing suicide, which would ruin the economy, and
about how profoundly sad the lyrics to that old song

"Red Rubber Ball" are ("The roller-coaster ride we took is nearly at an end / I bought my ticket with my tears, that's all I'm gonna spend"), and we talked about the similar chemical composition of tears and seawater, of tears and great diluvial catastrophes, and about the tears of feckless, moribund men in frilly aprons, and how the brutal indifference of time was like a vast inexorable army of locusts, and how there'd been 10^{26} nanoseconds since the Big Bang...

Given all the cosmic aperçus and trippy metaphysical speculation we'd indulge in for hours on end, you'd think we were high, except we *weren't* high. Y'know? We were just sitting there.

Anyway...the Imaginary Intern thought that the whole video-game idea—this whole thing about a first-person shooter fighting his way back to his mother's uterus and unraveling the DNA in the zygote—was completely dope. *But,* he had serious, emphatic reservations about what that entailed for me. He didn't think I really wanted to get involved with this sort of rigid chronology of pivotal incidents (even one that was retrograde). He thought I would so much prefer a more associative approach to autobiography, whatever that might be.

"I know you," he said. "And whether you're going backwards or forwards, you're still obliging yourself to hew to this strict chronology, and, trust me, this is not something you're going to really want to do."

So, it was the Imaginary Intern's idea that, though

Gone with the Mind should probably still be somehow in the form of a first-person shooter game, it should take place at a mall...with some kind of mall shooter peering through the crosshairs of a telescopic gun scope. And I don't remember the exact conversation, but I do recall him suggesting to me that even if it ultimately turned out that I retained only some vague vestige of the video-game idea, I needed to actually sit down and play a video game—something I hadn't really ever done (with the exception of arcade games like Ms. Pac-Man and Donkey Kong years ago).

So I went out, purchased an Xbox, bought myself a copy of Call of Duty: Black Ops II, and, uh...it didn't take me long to realize that I was astonishingly, exasperatingly terrible at it...I mean seriously, terminally inept at it...I could not, no matter how many times I tried, get beyond the most rudimentary level, and after about a week, thoroughly disgusted with myself, I just gave up and never played it or any other video game again, ever again. But I've maintained an abiding, avid interest in video games—just in theory, not in practice. I'm really in love with this whole idea—this sort of mythic and, to me, exemplary notion—of a new breed of cultural intelligentsia comprised of maladjusted, *otaku* kids holed up in their tiny bedrooms in Nagasaki or wherever, subsisting on Hot Pockets and Red Bull, inventing games, producing music, making films, whatever...this idea that our culture is now generated by disaffected, socially phobic kids who won't come out of their rooms. It obviously resonates with me because I tended to be such a bedroom recluse myself. One of my very favorite books is David Kushner's account of John Carmack and John Romero (the cocreators of Doom, that pioneering, classic first-person shooter series) entitled *Masters of Doom: How Two Guys Created an Empire and Transformed Pop Culture*…in fact, at one point, the Imaginary Intern and I wanted to call the autobiography *Gone with the Mind: How Two Guys, by the Inversion of a Single Letter—Simply by Turning One Letter Upside Down!—Transformed a 1939 Historical Epic Starring Clark Gable and Vivien Leigh into the Story of a Fey Little Demagogue with Blond Bangs on a Flying Balcony.* The ambivalent relationship I have with video games is actually very similar to the relationship I have with couture—it's all in theory and not at all in practice. I'm really fascinated by designers, but I have no interest in or, um…inclination to wear designer clothes myself. I just wear T-shirts and flannel pajama bottoms every day basically…some version of that. That said, I love Alicia Drake's book *The Beautiful Fall: Lagerfeld, Saint Laurent, and Glorious Excess in 1970s Paris.* And I couldn't wait to see Bertrand Bonello's film *Saint Laurent* when it opened at the New York Film Festival. And I've always been, unsurprisingly, extremely interested in Rei Kawakubo and in the Maison Martin Margiela, especially the way that everyone who worked at that particular atelier wore identical white lab coats…that kind of anonymity, that idea of eliminating any trace of individuality, and that kind of inclusively collaborative environment was very appealing to the Imaginary Intern and me. The way the ownership of ideas was shared equally by everyone was very much the way we wanted to work together. And we were actually toying around with this movie idea once about a fashion house very much like Maison Martin Margiela, except that it was also a cult...an apocalyptic cult like Heaven's Gate, that group in San Diego whose members all committed suicide (all of them wearing identical black shirts, sweatpants, and Nike Decade sneakers) so their souls could be picked up by a UFO trailing the Hale-Bopp comet (the UFO, their version, I suppose, of the flying balcony). And I'd written a scene that takes place during a very elaborate runway show that's situated in the summer palace of an eighteenth-century Russian tsar:

INT. SUMMER PALACE

Tsar Poet weeps into tear pots. Apes trot past. Servant brings silver platter with rat pesto on pre-toast. (Pre-toast is bread put in a toaster just long enough to warm it.)

And I read the scene to the Imaginary Intern, and I remember him saying, "Do you realize that *tsar poet, tear pots, apes trot, rat pesto,* and *pre-toast* are all anagrams of *prostate?*"

And I immediately realized that, without my having been consciously aware of it, the entire movie (although we never actually got much beyond those first few lines from that opening scene) was essentially about my recent bout with prostate cancer. (The robotic prostatectomy I underwent at Mount Sinai Hospital is what we—my mother and I—are referring to when we say, "On December 3, 2012, I was raped by a robot on the corner of Fifth Avenue and 101st Street in New York City.")

The Imaginary Intern wore a T-shirt that said *Amor Fati*—"love your fate." And he'd say, "Whatever happens to you, however degrading and humiliating and fucked up, you should appreciate it, because you can put it in the autobiography. So if no one comes to your reading, incorporate it, put it in."

I guess the jury's still out on whether or not anyone's "officially" here for the reading…I mean, since you two guys are here, and I'm reading…

PANDA EXPRESS WORKER
(Looks up from scrolling Tinder on his phone.)

What?

MARK

I said—I guess the jury's still out on whether or not you're "officially" here for the reading…since you're here, and I'm reading…

*   *   *

Y'know, something interesting just occurred to me...the Imaginary Intern once said something to me—I don't remember his exact words—but it was something that gave me the vague impression that he might have had a sort of *nostalgie de la boue* predilection for blue-collar workers and sailors...but aside from this one fleeting, enigmatic allusion (and I wish I could remember what it was that he said...it's possible it was in relation to that merry-go-round operator who tried to seduce my mother...when I told him that story...but I'm just not sure), nothing of the sort was ever overtly broached again. But I have to say, thinking about it right now, that in all the countless hours we'd sit on the couch and watch TV together, he never once said anything like "Hey, isn't that woman gorgeous?" or "Don't you think such-and-such an actress is hot?!" Though, on the other hand, he never evinced any kind of erotic enthusiasm for men on TV either. He was really all about the work, every single thing he saw he processed as potential fodder for the project. He was one of these to-tally...*esemplastic* kind of guys—y'know, he had a very synthetic, very practical and resourceful kind of sensibility, always about cobbling together the most disparate, miscellaneous things. We were watching some show once or some hockey game or something, and this Twizzlers commercial came on where everything in the world is made out of red Twizzlers—the cars, the highways, the bridges, the skyline, trees, the signage, the Statue of Liberty, Mount Rushmore, the hot-air balloons, everything—and this really, really impressed the Imaginary Intern and he said, "That's exactly what *Gone with the Mind* should be like! It should all be made out of the same thing!"

And I said it's a little like that commercial for Lay's potato chips where the Mr. Potato Head husband comes home from work and he says, "Sweetie, I'm home," but he can't find her, and he's looking all around, and finally catches his Potato Head wife clandestinely eating potato chips in this closet, this pantry...and he's appalled and he's like, "But you're a potato!" Here, it's a world all made of potatoes. It's potatoes eating potatoes.

And the Imaginary Intern said, "I don't know...that seems to me to be about nonprocreative desire, about autophagy as the apotheosis of self-love. The husband catches his wife in an act of masturbatory self-consumption and he's reflexively pissed about it, but then the last shot of the commercial reveals *both* of them in the closet eating the potato chips (i.e., masturbating), so...I think that's really about overcoming heteronormative shame, whereas Twizzlers World is all about monism. To me, it's all about turning everything into, or everything being made out of, a kind of unitary material...It's about all things originating from a single source. That's what I was saying before about *Gone with the Mind*...It should be all red Twizzlers."

I'm paraphrasing the Imaginary Intern, who was

extremely plainspoken...I mean, he never used any kind of academic or poststructuralist or psychoanalytic jargon...He expressed himself in a very, very simple, very childlike way, actually. In fact, he did a lot of phumphering, a lot of stammering...but in all his unguarded speech disfluencies, in all his uhs and ums, sometimes I thought I discerned some sort of encrypted content. My grandmother Rose (my dad's mom) was a blinker. She had this cute, coy way of blinking when she talked that always made me think of Betty Boop for some reason. I think that's probably why, when I was ten years old, I became so obsessed with that American POW who, during a televised press conference in North Vietnam, blinked his eyes in Morse code spelling out the word T-O-R-T-U-R-E. So I kind of suspected that the Imaginary Intern's uhs and ums constituted some kind of code too, but he left before I could determine what that code actually was, if there even was one in the first place. (My grandmother, who became very mischievous when she had even the slightest bit of alcohol, once told me that she saw a man climb into my mother's bedroom window when my father was away on a business trip about nine months before I was born. And she said that she suspected that this man was my real, biological father.

"What did this guy look like?" I asked her.

And she said, "He was a short, pudgy, mustachioed Italian man in a red shirt and blue overalls."

"Was he wearing a red cap, white gloves, and brown shoes?" I asked.

"Yeah," she said.

"And was there a red *M* in a white circle on the front of his hat and gold buttons on his overalls?"

"Yeah!"

And I was like, "Nana, that's Mario, from Super Mario Brothers, the video game."

And she gave me that double Betty Boop *blink-blink*.

Now that I think of it, it was a kind of feigned daffiness, a kind of playing dumb. She really was absolutely brilliant at playing dumb, a virtuoso, and she was capable of just driving people to distraction with that, particularly my dad. It never bothered me really, I just sort of went with it. In the last few years of her life, when she was living at a...what do you call those places?...not a nursing home...an assisted-living facility...on Ventura Boulevard in Studio City out in California...I used to call her every week or so, and she'd always ask me how my Mexican wife was, knowing full well that my wife, Mercedes, is Ecuadorean, not Mexican. But I'd just go with it and I'd tell her how she was doing. And once, I called her and, over the course of maybe an hour-long conversation, she insisted on speaking to me as if I were my dad's brother, my uncle Richie. And again, I just went along with it. But I knew that she knew it was me, because at one point she asked "Richie" how his Mexican wife was.)

While we were working on *Gone with the Mind*, I was extremely superstitious about anything remotely related to the book. I work out at the gym (NYSC on Fourteenth and Garden) every other day lifting weights and I run for about an hour or so along the Hudson River on my off days from the weight training, and the midpoint of my run is the train station, Hoboken Terminal, and there's a sign in stenciled letters on the windowpane of the door to the waiting room that reads:

WAITING ROOM
CLOSED BETWEEN
1:00 A.M.–5:30 A.M.
DAILY

And each and every single time I'd reach that door, panting and floridly OCD, I'd press the appropriate letters—as if I were keying in a password on an ATM touchscreen—to form the acronym for *Gone with the Mind:* The *g* in *Waiting,* the *w* in *Between,* the *t* in *Between,* and the *m* in *5:30 a.m.*

Also, if I made a decision about the book and within the next couple of hours I saw a woman's exposed armpit, I would take that to be a mystical ratification of that decision. (I'm not really talking about an armpit with encrypted content—more like a yea-saying armpit.) For example: Once, when I was in my early twenties, my father got drunk at a dinner party, and said something extremely cruel and derisive about me to a guest whom he very much admired and, I think, emulated to a significant degree—he was an advertising executive who was becoming very rich and politically influential. (He's dead now.) I was having a lot of problems at the time—feeling very unfulfilled, rootless, unactualized, unemployable, I guess feeling sort of worthless, and having all sorts of debilitating and undiagnosable and probably psychosomatic stomach ailments...so I was particularly vulnerable, and I remember thinking an instant after the slur came out of his mouth, *Hitler, where art thou?* I was so hurt and so exquisitely humiliated, and I remember thinking at that moment that if the Gestapo had shown up (we were living in West Orange, New Jersey, at the time) looking for Jews, I would have led them straight into the dining room and said, "There's a big one right there—the drunk guy playing the clarinet." (I remember this *so* clearly. Injured—in this case, *mutilated*—pride leaves extraordinarily eidetic, graven memories.) It was a singular aberration for my father, who's an extremely principled and scrupulously considerate person—none of which, I suppose, would make him immune to a mother-besotted boy's Oedipal fantasies of patricide. (In traditional folktales, the revenge of the father for his son's Oedipal ideation is, of course, to pass along to that son a genetic predisposition for prostate cancer, which is precisely what my father, in fact, did.) I can't remember my dad being either that drunk or unthinkingly nasty ever again. I, on the other hand, have been drunk and unthinkingly nasty thousands of times—a pattern which began when I was very young, like five. I had a big, nearly life-size stuffed orangutan that my uncle Richie had given me, with fur and a rubber face and hands and feet (I think my mom might have mentioned him in her introduction), and I'd prop him up next to me on my bed, and I'd pretend that we were at a bar together, and I'd sip from a bottle of Novahistine Elixir, a decongestant/antihistamine the color of green crème de menthe, until I was pretty fucked up. There were always bottles of it in my room because (as my mom said) I was prone to colds and earaches. This was obviously before the advent of child-resistant packaging and safety caps. And I remember I'd get very loud and very irascible and aggressive with the orangutan, and say some really awful, insulting things to him…it wasn't funny. It would start off amicably enough, my arm around his shoulders (the way I'd seen guys on TV do it), joking around, telling him stories, singing (mostly Civil War songs I'd learned from an album my parents had gotten me, "The Battle Hymn of the Republic," "When Johnny Comes Marching Home," "Just Before the Battle, Mother," things like that), but after a while my mood would sour, I'd take something the wrong way, a look, a completely innocuous gesture, and my temper would flare, and I'd end up flinging him down the stairs. In my memory, the orangutan sort of *floated* through the air—I don't know, maybe he had an unusually high lift-to-drag ratio for a stuffed animal or something—but he'd hit the floor at the bottom of the stairs with an awful thud, and my mother would come frantically running from wherever she was in the house, breathless and flushed, thinking I'd fallen down the stairs. (I never named the orangutan. I think even at that age I somehow intuitively understood that *all* names are slave names, that the absolute fixity of a name constitutes a form of captivity.)

For whatever reasons (discretion, embarrassment, etc.), I had very mixed feelings about including all of this in the book, but I thought it through and finally decided to put it in, and I went for a run, and the first thing I saw once I got out along the river was a woman with her arms raised as she gathered her hair into a ponytail with a scrunchie, exposing her armpits, which I took to be an unmistakable sign that including these anecdotes about my dad and the stuffed orangutan was absolutely the right thing to do.

I've had an armpit fetish since I was a boy, and I think its origin was this Modigliani painting of a recumbent woman with one arm lifted behind her head that was hung up on the wall in my childhood bedroom in Jersey City. There's the visual allure...the, uh...the, uh, *iconography* of that exemplary gesture of sexual surrender, of surrender to one's own pleasure...and then there's just the whole erotics, the appreciation, the connoisseurship...I'm trying to think of a word here that doesn't make it seem overly perverse...the *fondness* for the animal smells of the human body. In Elizabethan times, lovers would stay in touch by exchanging peeled apples which had been soaked in their armpit sweat before they parted company. Napoleon famously wrote

Josephine from one of his military campaigns, "I will return to Paris tomorrow evening. Don't wash." And An-
ton Chekhov wrote, "I don't understand anything about
the ballet; all I know is that during the intervals the bal-
lerinas stink like horses." Well, I don't understand anything about Chekhov, but I can only assume he meant
that approvingly. And I was watching the reality show
Couples Therapy on VH1 the other night, and there was
this whole poolside conversation between Jenna Jameson and her boyfriend, MMA-trainer John Wood, about
men's fixations on women's armpits.

So, it's not just me.

There was a woman at my gym who would work out
and get very sweaty, and I loved the way she smelled.
It reminded me a little of Wite-Out, and also that smell
when you open the flip top of a can of new tennis
balls...I didn't really run into her that frequently, but
this one day I walked into the gym and there she was
working out...on a tricep machine, I think...and I
really, really wanted to get on that machine as soon as
she was done with it...while her scent was still in the
air. I don't know if that sounds creepy or not, but I'm
just being honest here, I'm really being, like, *totally* nonfictional. Anyhow...she finishes up, and she's about to
clean the seat and the, uh...the arm pads, or whatever
you call them...

"You don't have to do that," I said.

"I'm really gross," she said, an assertion which obviously only served to inflame me further.

And, in order to prevent her from wiping it down with one of those antiseptic towelettes, I threw myself across the apparatus, as one would shield a tree from a chain saw.

And one of those idiotic trainers came over, one of those little meatballs with a clipboard, and he asked her if she wanted to lodge a complaint with the manager, etc., etc.

And out the corner of my eye, I noticed this guy in his mid-sixties whom I recognized immediately as the psychiatrist I'd gone to a few times after my prostate cancer surgery. He was working out sort of perfunctorily with a set of very light kettlebells. I hadn't seen him for years, and I had no idea he even belonged to my gym. He's a gaunt, pockmarked man with a gold incisor, who, when I used to see him in his office (on Eleventh and University), always wore very beautiful, very elegant bespoke suits. So it was more than a little jarring to see him so incongruously casual in baggy red nylon shorts and a Jiffy Lube T-shirt. Seeing him again made me remember the first thing I told him in that initial visit—a story about how, when I was in the second grade, at James F. Murray No. 38 Elementary School on Stegman Parkway back in Jersey City, I swindled some color-blind classmate I was supposed to be sharing crayons with out of all the brightly colored ones, giving him basically just the browns and the blacks, because I knew he couldn't really tell the difference. And I confided to the psychiatrist that ever since then I've thought of myself as an almost pathologically selfish, sort of monstrous human being. And I remember him just sitting there and not saying anything at all in response, and then I told him that since my surgery, I've had a very disturbing recurrent nightmare in which surgical robots go wild and stalk the countryside, tearing out men's prostates. And I remember him staring down at his notes, and saying that my dream reminded him of Vincent Bugliosi's description of members of the Manson Family (specifically Susan Atkins, Patricia Krenwinkel, and Tex Watson) as "heartless, bloodthirsty robots." And then he finally looked up at me and said, "You don't really strike me as either a bloodthirsty robot or a monstrous human being."

So I turned to this trainer with the clipboard and—in the way that one sometimes distractedly blurts out something from a reverie that doesn't quite but, in a weird way, almost perfectly suits present circumstances—said, "I'm not a robot, I'm a human being," a fact which, by the way, I'm not particularly proud of. But *that* whole can of worms—cyborgs, prosthetics, DIY synthetic biology, techno-sodomy, posthumanism, whether one's aggregate self, one's "mind," can be downloaded—is something that I'm planning on dealing with ad nauseam in the excerpts I'll be reading tonight. For now, if you're wondering what fragrances a withdrawn fifty-eight-year-old man, who still confides primarily in stuffed animals, action figures, and his mother, wears: my three current scents are: for writing, Jo Malone Vetyver; for the gym, L'Eau de Jatamansi by L'Artisan

Parfumeur; and for going out at night (e.g., to the mall), Bois d'Arménie by Guerlain.

I don't know if you guys can smell me from way over there...

(The PANDA EXPRESS WORKER and the SBARRO WORKER are ignoring all this completely.)

MARK

We (the Imaginary Intern and I) used to talk a lot about an olfactory art, some kind of postlinguistic, pheromonal medium that would be infinitely more nuanced than language (and without language's representational deficiencies), a purely molecular syntax freed from all the associative patterns and encoded, ideological biases of language, that could produce the revelatory sensations of art by exciting chemosensory neurons instead of the "mind," that could jettison all the incumbent imperial narratives and finally get to something *really* nonfictional. And we both tremendously admired Helen Keller's militantly pro-olfactory polemic "Smell, the Fallen Angel" in her book *The World I Live In*. And we both agreed that if all the highly anticipated virtual- and augmented-reality technologies turn out to be just based on sight and sound, they'll be complete dead ends. And we both thought that *Diners, Drive-Ins and Dives* or *Beat Bobby Flay*, which are predicated upon olfaction and gustation, are more sophisticated shows epistemologically than, say, something like *Bill Moyers Journal* or *Charlie Rose*, which are based on archaic discursive practices. And we both felt very strongly—for a completely different reason (basically because *Baylisascaris procyonis* worms and *Schistosoma mansoni* flukes are infinitely more interesting characters than advertising executives or a police commissioner)—that *Monsters Inside Me* (the Animal Planet documentary series about parasites) is a better show than probably anything else on television.

Not sure about any of this, just throwing it out there...but this all seems to represent a fairly radical revision of Descartes, whose "I think, therefore I am" becomes instead "I stink, therefore I think."

Right?

There are smells that your own body produces that can have the same effect as Proust's madeleine, producing that extraordinary, unbidden gust of remembrance, the *mémoire involontaire*. I once mentioned this in passing to the Imaginary Intern, adding that I was reluctant to talk about it because I thought people might think it's juvenile or gross, and he said, "No, no, no, dude...you should *absolutely* talk about it, it's something so many people can identify with," which is such a totally Imaginary Intern thing to say, by the way—he was so perspicacious about things like this, but without even the slightest bit of self-importance or pretension. I, on the other hand, have always been squeamish and neurotically reticent about things like this, but I do think it's particularly pertinent here: there's a certain bowel movement of mine—and it's not something I can reduplicate at will; I've yet to figure out what food or combination of foods actually produces it—whose smell immediately transports me back in time to a very specific men's room at the Deal Casino, a beach club in Deal, New Jersey, that my family frequented during summers when I was a little kid. This was a very lovely and carefree, very richly experienced, almost psychedelically vibrant time in my life (a time when I first saw zeppelins in the sky, first heard the sound of mah-jongg tiles being shuffled, first caught glimpses of naked Marlboro smoking middle-aged women in cabanas, etc.) and that particular fecal smell, and the memories it instantly evokes, buoys me for hours and sometimes days on end, and it's something that probably got me through my almost unassuageable grief when the Imaginary Intern left, and I'd sit there on the toilet desperately hoping to reconjure his face from the configuration of cracks in the tile floor.

I think I mentioned before all his elaborate variations on my own motifs, which seemed to me so much more brilliant than the original ideas...Well, after he suddenly left—which I'll talk about more in a minute—in my grief, in my anguished disbelief (which almost immediately exposed long-repressed memories of my dead sister and swelled into a pain of infinite yearning that's never quite abated), I ransacked the house in search of any remnants of him, and I found a trove of his "poems," which were not originally intended as poems at all, I suppose, but were simply artless collations of my own fragmentary notes, but which have the numinous, elegiac, oracular quality (in my opinion, at least) of the greatest poetry, of, say, a Friedrich Hölderlin or, uh...of a Gérard de Nerval...whose disdain for the material world matched that of the Imaginary Intern ("This life is a hovel and a place of ill-repute. I'm ashamed that God should see me here"), who famously walked his pet lobster Thibault at the end of a blue silk ribbon through the gardens of the Palais-Royal, and who hanged himself from a sewer grating in the rue de la Vieille-Lanterne with an apron string he believed to be the Queen of Sheba's garter. As the Imaginary Intern would say, you can't make this stuff up...which, come to think of it, is a sort of ironic thing for an Imaginary Intern to say.

In a very literal sense, the Imaginary Intern existed for the project—he was all about the project...all about the production of *Gone with the Mind*, that was his sole remit, as they say. So, thanks largely to him, everything we talked about, no matter how seemingly extraneous or irrelevant—Twizzlers commercials, the molecular basis of infrared detection by pit vipers, Betty Boop, Helen Keller, Jenna Jameson, parasitic worms, whatever— somehow or other wound its way back to our work. The only exception to this, the only thing we didn't treat in a utilitarian way, the only thing that was completely sacrosanct, was the epic, heroic role the Soviet Union played in the defeat of Nazi Germany in World War II, and, in particular, the defense of Stalingrad.

One afternoon, I got back home from the gym and he was gone. I found a note he'd left behind entitled "Ciao":

One just keeps saying, "No...No...No..."
Head bowed, hat in hand,
A cringing, cunning little step back,
With each dialectical evasion,
Retreating, receding, "no...no...no..."
Until one simply disappears...

I miss, so terribly, working on *Gone with the Mind* with him. And I miss the times when we'd just sit around, listening to music together in the dark (usually moody, British postpunk pop) or watching TV.

Life's a harrowing fucking slog—we're driven by irrational, atavistic impulses into an unfathomable void of quantum indeterminacy—but, still... it's nice to have a friend, a comrade, a paracosm, whatever, to share things with.

The earliest folktales tended to be about single-cell organisms which lived deep below the surface of the earth, where temperatures routinely exceeded one hundred degrees Fahrenheit. Soon, though, folktales began to feature tiny multicellular worms which had evolved to survive in the extreme, inhospitable conditions of the subsurface biosphere. These worms—belonging to "the vast and diverse phylum of nematodes"—ate bacteria and often grew no bigger than two-hundredths of an inch. Then, for a very, very long period of time after this, almost all folktales pivoted around a cobbler, his fat, conniving wife, and their gullible daughter. But the degree of refinement was extraordinarily high, each ensuing folktale an almost imperceptibly subtle modification of its predecessor. Today, these elegant algorithms have given way to *autobiography*, with the hope that it might carry the same breadth of allegorical signification.

So were I to say something like...I don't know... something like...and I'm just riffing here, I'm just freestyling...something like..."I was a delicate little boy with flaxen bangs from Jersey City, who was alternately titillated and revolted by other children my age...those, those filthy, cross-eyed children in Jughead whoopee caps who'd run around screaming at the tops of their lungs with long pink roundworms wriggling out their nostrils...and my pretty, my pretty young mother—she was *so* young then!—in her, in her, her pink Izod polo shirt and her short, khaki wraparound skirt and her penny loafers—would prepare me a lunch of cream of mushroom soup, with banana Turkish taffy for dessert, and she'd read aloud folktales about other delicate little boys *just like me* (whose pretty mothers *also* read to them as they ate), exertions which would leave her almost too exhausted to fend off the coarse advances of the stooped, hook-nosed peddlers and the, uh…the sweaty merry-go-round operators who seemed to be endlessly ringing our doorbell"…something like that…I think you could discern in even something like that, certain folkloric elements, certain of the, the, uh…the generic narratemes that the Soviet folklorist Vladimir Propp enumerated…And even though the lexicon (Jughead, Turkish taffy) and the clothes (the Izod polo shirts, the penny loafers) clearly situates it in a very specific time, in a relatively contemporaneous reality (the early sixties), there's still, to my mind at least, an *illud tempus* (to borrow Eliade's phrase) suggested here…a kind of, uh…a vaguely medieval, once-upon-a-time-ness suggested by these roving peddlers and those caterwauling, parasite-infested children…We are—all of us—so deeply, so atavistically inculcated with the structures and the tropes that inhere in the very act of storytelling, that no sooner do we begin narrating our own presumably unprecedented childhoods, than we—no matter who we are—reflexively conjure up the very same brigands and woodsmen, the very same vagabonds and troubadours and ogres, the very same hermits and sly, anthropomorphic animals, or recognize their interchangeable avatars whom we have inescapably become, through the telling and the retelling…And I think you're going to find in some of the excerpts I'm planning on reading tonight…and right now I can just pick arbitrarily a couple of lines off the top of my head, lines like "I was fascinated by the nuns who seemed to float across the boulevard on rainy afternoons," for instance…or, uh…"I got my first hand job from a schizophrenic girl with webbed fingers"…or even in a passing recollection like—and I don't remember the exact words off the top of my head here—something like "I'm pacing outside the club, smoking a cigarette, it's like mid-January and I'm fucking freezing in this filthy Trix T-shirt, one of those little blue dental bibs with the metal-ball chains, red plaid flannel pajama bottoms with this giant hole in the crotch, and a pair of white clogs…and my father calls to tell me that he's surprised I hadn't been included in Philip Roth's list of 'formidable postwar writers'" or…or even in a section that appears toward the very end of the autobiography where I say something like "I'm fifty-eight years old, and I'd still rather try to support myself by mowing people's lawns and babysitting than by teaching" or, uh—and this is one of the last lines in the whole book—"Would it be so terrible for a man who perseveres under the Damoclean threat of cancer and the ever-present specter of assassination to simply try and have one last meal with his old mother in the food court of a mall?" I think even in these lines, you can find a sense of the *fantastic*…a sense of fairy-tale enchantment…But that idea of enchantment, as we move through the second decade of the twenty-first century, seems ever more adulterated, ever more degraded…and, one wonders, by what exactly? As chronologies of diagnosis and treatment replace the surrealist poetry of our symptomology, how quickly it can all begin to seem like a PowerPoint presentation at a TED talk or the strobe-effect of PTSD flashbacks in a Lifetime movie...

Of course the battle between the materialist rationalists and the anti-materialist irrationalists is long over, and the anti-materialist irrationalists lost, and we await our UFOs and our flying balconies to come and bear us away.

The chorus in Seneca's *Thyestes* asks: "Will the last days come in our time?" And I would say, Yes, absolutely. I mean, the last days might very well come during this reading tonight. I think my mom mentioned before that the floodwaters are rising, right? And assassins, *onryōs* (vengeful spirits), first-person shooters...mall shooters, whatever you want to call them...are all wandering around, floating around. And I don't think any of this should especially disturb anyone. I don't think it's anything to get all bummed out about. I think it should actually make everyone feel really good. Oprah said to Lindsay Lohan: "Vultures are waiting to pick your bones...that should *liberate* you." Someone in the video game Total War: Shogun 2 says something to the effect of: "a samurai should not scandalize his name by holding his one and only life too dear." In other words, the true samurai enters the battle with no thought of return. And I really think that's how you have to look at it when you do a nonfiction reading, when you really commit to only presenting empirically verifiable material, when you're really *deadly* serious about that. And I bring up the Japanese writer Yukio Mishima now, not because he was a sickly, pale, pampered introvert of a child who grew up to become obsessed with bodybuilding and who, as an adult, when his mother complained that "Mommy's foot hurts," proceeded to lick the sore area in front of friends and family, but because he gave, on November 25, 1970, one of the best nonfiction readings ever given when he stepped out onto a balcony (not the flying balcony of the Palazzo Venezia, but a balcony nonetheless) and declaimed a prepared manifesto to several hundred soldiers gathered below who mocked and jeered him (and who, by the way, weren't officially "there for the reading" either), returned inside, disemboweled himself, and was then beheaded by a member of his private militia. I'm qualifying this by calling it one of the *best* nonfiction readings ever given. It could have been one of the *great* nonfiction readings ever given if Mishima's mother, Shizue Hiraoka, had been there, but she wasn't (although she did attend his funeral). I mean, you'd have to say—and I think this is *so* obvious given the fact that being mocked, jeered at, and martyred in the presence of one's mom is the key, the key ingredient here—that Christ on the Cross (in the presence, of course, of his mother, the Virgin Mary) gave one of the greatest nonfiction readings ever given.

Now, I just want to fast-forward six hours or so in the Gospel narrative to make a small point. The Virgin

Mary was *not* a Ferbering mother. And though the life-less body of Christ did not literally cry out for her, the exigencies of Christian doctrine surely did. And un-like *my* mom on those unfortunate nights alluded to earlier, Mary did respond, and unlike *my* mom, Mary cradled *her* son in her arms ... and hence the enormously popular, endlessly reproduced, and invariably eroticized image of the Pietà. Now, in all fairness, we can't un-derestimate the influence on young mothers—and my mom was only, what, barely twenty at that time?—we can't underestimate the ... the enormous influence of pro-Ferbering authorities like Dr. Spock who, when it came to children's sleep problems—and this may sur-prise you guys—was more draconian than even Ferber himself.

(The PANDA EXPRESS WORKER and the SBARRO WORKER are paying absolutely no attention to anything MARK is saying.)

MARK

But the simple truth of it is that if you take a certain type of boy with an extremely delicate temperament and you turn his bedroom into a dark, terrifying sort of prison cell (even if it's only for a couple of nights), a significant amount of self-radicalization is going to occur with *that* type of child in *that* type of environment. I still suffer, to this day, from an intractable compulsion to fold things into thirds instead of halves, which I believe is directly attributable to the Ferbering.

Okay, you guys might be thinking to yourselves, *how does Christ on the Cross constitute a nonfiction reading?* The Seven Statements from the Cross ("Father, forgive them, for they do not know what they do," "Truly, I say to you, today you will be with Me in paradise," "Woman, behold your son. Son, behold your mother," etc.) were extemporaneous utterances, they were not recited from any kind of pre-prepared text, so how is that a reading? To which I would say, very simply, that for a divine being like Jesus Christ, all of history— from the beginning ("word one") through eternity— has already been inscribed. All of it has already been written. To a divine being, it's all already a book, or a script, whatever. So, anything a divinity says, any seemingly spontaneous utterance He or She might make, constitutes a *reading.*

As I look out tonight, there are no Roman soldiers...but there are empty chairs to mock me. And some sort of...some sort of, at least virtual martyrdom impends; I can feel that in my bones. And my mom is right here, and I appreciate that tremendously. And so, I'm very proud tonight to be here at the Nonfiction at the Food Court Reading Series. And as I look out at my mother right now, eating pork fried rice out of a Styrofoam shell from Panda Express, I can't help but be reminded of when that teacher at James F. Murray No. 38 Elementary School in Jersey City used to hold me up to the window to show me that my mom was waiting for me outside in the schoolyard, to reassure me, to demonstrate to me that she hadn't "abandoned" me again, as I apparently felt she had during her second pregnancy. I guess like a lot of kids that age, I'd occasionally fabricate the vocations of my parents, and I remember once telling that particular teacher that my father, an attorney in Jersey City, was—and I'm paraphrasing here, I don't remember my exact words—that he was actually a tropical agronomist who specialized in diseases of the banana, perhaps a sly Oedipal dig at his virility. I remember the teacher smiling at that. She was a very smiley, very accommodating woman. But I always suspected that her smile was a mask. To me, even at that tender age—I think I was six—it suggested a latent misery, hidden by a great labor of repression and dissimulation. But as I look out at my mom tonight... Y'know, Heraclitus said, "No man ever steps in the same river twice, for it's not the same river and he's not the same man." But I also think that no son sees the same mother twice, for it's not the same mother and he's not the same son. So as I look out at my mom tonight, I see not only a woman with a unique sociocultural history as a daughter, as a mother, as a grandmother, a woman with an autobiography of her own, but I also see a techno-organic aggregate body that is bacterial, fungal, mineral, metal, electrochemical, digitally informational, etc., and then, if I put on these reading glasses, which help me a lot with close-range vision, but pretty seriously degrade my ability to focus on anything in the distance, I see a sort of flat, two-dimensional, distorted female figure composed of splintered planes, and then the more I squint through the reading glasses, the more she now seems reduced to a purely geometric abstraction, a vertical element perpendicular to a horizontal element, and she's achieved an object's phenomenological status as a thing prior to any meaning...and if I look through them like this—backwards—she seems to disaggregate completely. She becomes an exploded diagram of herself. Like the instructions you get with furniture from Ikea. And here the intelligible dimensions of the mother are extended into infinite space—the macroscopic realm of celestial bodies and the vast distances between them, and the intimate realm of microscopic organisms and cells. And the image of the mother as exploded diagram is, of course, the image of the mother as suicide bomber.

On May 28, 2013, I tweeted: *Spent the weekend just wandering around outside, caramelizing things with my crème brûlée torch.*

And then on August 28, 2014, I tweeted: *Just learned this morning that my Imaginary Intern is an ethnic Chechen.* I was being facetious, of course, and I wasn't sure if the Imaginary Intern had even seen the tweet, because we were both very busy that morning, off doing our separate things. I think he was reviewing and archiving childhood crayon drawings and digitized 8-millimeter birthday-party footage that my dad had shot in the early sixties, and I was, uh...you know what?...I think this

was a period of time when I'd become, like, mildly obsessed with Spaten lager beer . . . so I'm pretty sure that
that day I was out looking for a place that sold it by
the case. But it turned out that he had indeed seen the
tweet, because once the two of us reconvened later that
evening, he asked me, "What ethnicity do you actually
think I am?" And I don't remember exactly what I said,
probably something like, "Oh, you're a paracosm." Or
"Oh, you're a quasi-autonomous notional entity." Or
"You're an apparition from Figmentistan." Or something like that. Just kidding around with him. And I
remember he said, very seriously, "I think I'm a teratoma." And it took me a minute before I realized he
was alluding to an incident that had occurred, I don't
know, some fifteen years ago when my mom had an
ovarian cystic teratoma removed. I didn't know what a
teratoma was at the time, so I did some research and
I discovered that it's a kind of tumor that can contain
hair and teeth and, in rare cases, eyes and feet, but
much more commonly the hair and teeth, so I went out
and bought a tiny comb and a tiny toothbrush (I think
they were from a set of toiletries for one of those Troll
dolls that I found at a Toys "R" Us) and I gave them
to my mom at the hospital. And I immediately regretted the "gift" — I'd originally thought it was sort of cute
and clever in a completely innocuous way, but then it
just seemed like a creepy morbid attempt at humor at
her expense, and I was really apprehensive that she'd be
hurt and angry. And she so easily could have hobbled

me with a glare or a pained aversion of her eyes if she'd wanted to...because I don't think it was funny to her at all...I mean, she had two huge heliotrope bruises— one from a tourniquet they'd used to start the IV drip in her arm and one from a catheter she'd had on the dorsum of her hand—that made me wince when I looked at them, she was still nauseous from the anesthesia, and she was still in a considerable amount of pain from the surgery itself. But she just smiled at me, in that beautiful, gracious, indulgent way she has of smiling at me, the way she's always smiled at me. This is the Noh mask of her immutable benevolence.

I said a little while ago when I was talking about how my mom drove me to the mall tonight that I don't really like to talk to her when she's been drinking and she's driving over ninety miles an hour, because I don't want to distract her. And I was just being facetious. And it was a glib, thoughtless thing to say. Just for cheap laughs at her expense. And I just want to say that my mom does not drink and drive. And as soon as I said what I said, I regretted it completely. And, Mom, I looked over at you and you could have just glowered at me, which would have ruined the whole reading for me, the whole night...but you didn't. You just took it in stride. You just looked up at me, and smiled that beautiful, indulgent, luminous smile of yours, and went right back to your pork fried rice.

One stands up here, on a table in the middle of a food court, as one would upon a balcony overlooking a piazza thronged with swooning Fascists. And one becomes heedless, one becomes disinhibited, indiscreet...and one says all sorts of things one shouldn't say—

(MARK'S MOM, as if on cue, reaches furtively across the table to snare MARK'S egg roll.)

MARK

Don't eat mine, Mom.

(MARK and his MOM exchange a conspiratorial wink, as if this whole little pas de deux about the drunk driving, the ovarian tumor, and the egg roll had been predesigned to finally coax a reaction—any reaction—from the PANDA EXPRESS WORKER, who simply shrugs indifferently...whatever.)

MARK

I think one of the first things I ever wrote was a puppet play. Not a play that was intended to be performed *using* puppets, but a play intended to be performed *for* puppets—for an audience of puppets—for the stuffed animals and action figures in my bedroom. (So, given the fact that I still think that the ideal audience for my work is inanimate objects, a roomful of empty chairs actually constitutes a full house!) These plays, these productions, performances, whatever you want to call them, sort of bounced back and forth between dialogue and dance, and they were mounted in my room, as I said, and the audience would typically consist of my stuffed orangutan, maybe a G.I. Joe or two, and several dozen plastic Civil War soldiers. Many of the topics at play in these early works were those with which I'd been fixated since I was a little boy: Pietà sculptures, claustrophilia, fascism, flagellate protozoa, androgenized female Eastern European athletes, the fragility of persona, etc. And, as I said, there was dance. The choreography was spare, rudimentary. There were two basic movements that I'd perform simultaneously as I recited my monologues. I suppose in the way a sensitive child, say, in the Middle Ages, might see the threshing motions of men and women harvesting grain in the fields and make from that a formalized dance movement, a sweep of the arm could represent the eternal rhythm of the seasons, I repurposed two motions I'd seen adults perform many times in the milieu I grew up in. The first was a shifting of weight from my right foot to my left foot, back to my right, then to my left, back and forth and back and forth—this was a particular kind of swaying or *shuckling* I'd gleaned watching men preparing to hit a golf ball at the driving range or at an actual course. The other movement derives from women shuffling mahjongg tiles. I would extend my arms out in front of my body, palms down, and make circles with my hands, flat, horizontal circles, clockwise with my left hand, counterclockwise with my right. I'd perform these movements as I recited my stammering, maudlin soliloquies and the rabid harangues to my plastic soldiers. I guess this was a kind of, of…what's the word?…a kind of…*liminal* gesturing, a gesturing that announced that we were about to cross a threshold…that we were waiting…not knowing what's next…not knowing what violence or calamity my words might bring down upon us…This was my little *Totentanz*…my little dance of death… something along those lines, I guess…And I loved putting on these plays very, very much, alone in my room, with my rapt audience of inanimate aficionados. And, honestly, I never wanted to do "more" with it…or become "known" for it…or pursue it as, y'know, any kind of vocation or career.

Which reminds me of something interesting…Soon after the Imaginary Intern left, I found a postcard from him. There was a photograph on one side…it was a close-up of a white skinhead and behind him was this black guy (whose face and torso were out of frame) sort of standing over him, straddling him, so that his penis was lying down the center of the skinhead's shaved white skull, giving him, like, a penis Mohawk. And under the photograph was a caption that had originally read *Stay relevant*. But the Imaginary Intern had added, I guess with a Sharpie or something, the prefix *ir-* in front of the word *relevant*, so it read *Stay irrelevant*, meaning— at least this is my interpretation—don't do anything, whether it's having a friend drape his dick across your head or putting on little, sort of experimental USO performances for your plastic Civil War soldiers, or whatever—for the sake of becoming well known. Do the contrary. Cultivate your irrelevance, cultivate your gratuitousness. The Imaginary Intern had also stapled a clipping to the blank side of the postcard, presumably from some scientific journal like *Nature* or *Cell,* which had the headline "South Korean Microbiologist Discovers That Even Amoebae Fall into the Five Basic Archetypal Categories: Nerd, Bully, Hot, Dumpy, and New Kid," the meaning of which, with regard to that photograph, I'm still trying to understand, even though I realize it's entirely possible that he just stapled the clipping to the postcard as a way of saving the clipping—in other words, that he was just looking for something to staple the clipping to in order to file it, and just randomly grabbed the postcard, so that its contents were completely irrelevant. But I really, really doubt that, just given the way the Imaginary Intern seemed to deliberately generate—well, not *generate*... *locate* would probably be a better word—the way he seemed to very deliberately, very painstakingly, very precisely and rigorously *locate* signification in just about everything he did. But it's a precision and rigor that only becomes apparent in retrospect. In fact, I would say 99 percent of things involving the Imaginary Intern only become apparent in retrospect. And he really did fervently believe—as do I—in this whole idea of staying secret, of shunning the spotlight. A friend of mine once suggested that someone make a documentary about the Imaginary Intern...set up cameras all over the house like in that movie *Paranormal Activity*...and I told the Imaginary Intern about it, and he freaked. He hated the idea...And I immediately regretted having told him about it. It was a huge mistake. And sometimes I think that that's actually why he left. He just wanted to be completely off the radar, left alone, completely inconspicuous, completely off camera...I don't know if he'd been abused in his life or what...but he just wanted to be able to relax and act as loony and as dorky as he wanted to without having to worry about what anyone else thought, and I think the idea of a documentary just really shook him up, it really spooked him. I think I mentioned before that I've tried to re-conjure his face from the configuration of cracks in the tile floor of other bathrooms. In fact, I was sitting on the toilet in the men's room in the Nordstrom in this mall actually, and I thought I discerned his face in some craquelure on the floor, and I remember I was concentrating so hard on it, trying so hard to force a jumble of disparate features into a recognizable physiognomy, that I was actually straining, y'know, pressing in that way that can cause hemorrhoids, so I had to stop. I've had that sudden, that sudden frisson, that jolt of *It's him!* many times, and I'll squint and I'll look from different angles and inevitably it's a false alarm, it's not him...and it's...it's a big, big letdown, it really is...it's a shitty feeling.

But that's what nonfiction is, people. Shitty feelings

and encounters with death. And that's why we're here tonight.

The Imaginary Intern once defined *autobiography* as "a compulsion to share one's life with strangers on social media." Along with this compulsion comes a burden of truth...Hölderlin wrote in his poem "Patmos," "The lords are kind, but while they reign / what they most abhor is falsehood."...And so, in honor of all the martyrs who've died keeping it real, I'd just really like to set the record straight about my mom's driving—not only does she not drink and drive, she barely drinks at all, and she's a *terrific* driver...just a really, *really* great driver.

And what I mean about honoring all the martyrs who've died keeping it real is that people make enormous sacrifices writing nonfiction instead of fiction. I mean, I could have easily concocted something a lot more interesting than an ovarian cystic teratoma for my mom, if that's what I wanted to do. I could have given her a tumor that...that...I don't know...a tumor that could sing and dance and act and do impersonations like Sammy Davis Jr. or something. And everyone would have said, "Oh, that's *so* cool. How'd you ever think of that? Where do you get your ideas?" Y'know? And as for me—prostate cancer? I mean, *c'mon.* Prostate cancer has got to be the most boring cancer there is. Seriously. *So* many men have prostate cancer. If I'd really wanted to give myself some fascinating, bizarre disease, I certainly could have just used my imagination and come up with something...like some weird...I don't know...some grotesque prolapse or exotic anal fissure that has to be treated with habanero-infused flushable wipes, and everyone would have been like, "Oh my God, magical realism! That's so cool!" And some people would have been like, "What are you on?" And I could have shot back with Lance Armstrong's "What am I on? I'm on my bike, busting my ass six hours a day. What are *you* on?" In other words, I don't have an exotic anal fissure. And my mom didn't have an ovarian tumor that could sing and dance and play the drums and that had one eye. And that's not what we're all here for tonight at the Nonfiction at the Food Court Reading Series. Tonight's about reality. Tonight we say death to fiction. And by *fiction* we mean anything (or anyone) that occludes the forces that really matter. And we also say— and this is something the Imaginary Intern and I used to say to each other before bed:

Death to anyone who opposes the negation of everything that causes us to be dead while alive.

And I just want to say again that I'm extremely proud to have been invited. And, y'know, something occurred to me in the car on the way over here tonight, and it's that we're all—each and every one of us— ticking time bombs, potential first-person shooters, mall shooters, whatever...who, given the opportunity to cast off the constraints of petit bourgeois morality, would choose random sadomasochistic chem-sex with hooded strangers over real relationships any day of the week. We live in this crazy, inside-out, totally bizarro world today where, just to give you another example, several large-scale Phase III clinical trials have apparently confirmed the efficacy of fecal transplants in the treatment of social-anxiety disorder. I have a friend who's a psychiatrist, and I called him recently because I'd been wondering about whether my fondness for chubby women with small breasts was somehow homoerotic—not that it's something I'm overly concerned about or anything, I was just curious to see what his professional opinion was—and at some point in the conversation he mentioned tangentially the, uh...the funny thing about the fecal transplants.

Look—yes, life is super-trippy. Yes, it may contain intense violence, blood/gore, sexual content, and/or strong language that may not be suitable for children, on-screen defecation, long strings of snot, and sad, sad times...

But, again, I just want to say this:

Nothing else in my life compares to the vitality and plenitude of this moment right now, right here. For me, these plastic chairs and tables are as real an audience as the miners and cowboys Oscar Wilde regaled in Leadville, Colorado, in 1882, or the insensible drunks at the saloon who jeered Granville Thorndyke, the traveling thespian in John Ford's *My Darling Clementine:* "To die, to sleep; / To sleep: perchance to dream"...

Oh Thorndyke, you preposterous, undaunted

poseur...ever posing as the sad, sad, Ferbered prince...
Oh sad, sad, Ferbered prince...sad, sad, Ferbered, oedi-
pally conflicted, impotent prince and poseur...ever posing autobiographically as yourself.

As any mother-besotted son knows, especially the
mother-besotted son who is unassimilable in the milieu
of his contemporaries, the presence of the mother is simply the cruel betokening of her absence. The mother is
the irreducible lack, the hole at the center of it all. And
even when we are flying *from* that, we are flying *toward* it.

I've always thought of my childhood as Edenic, as a
distinct kind of paradise (and my adulthood as an expul-
sion, as a fall), and I still think of Jersey City (circa 1960)
as the loveliest place in the world, I still think of it as...as
paradigmatically beautiful, with its prewar apartments
and Beaux-Arts office buildings, and its pastel, beatific
twilights...and infested, as it was, with nuns. And I
used to tell people, when I got a little older, that my
parents were very much like Rob and Laura Petrie on
The Dick Van Dyke Show...very young, sophisticated, very
good-looking...although I never really identified much
with their son, Richie, who was much too rambunctious and coarse for me. I guess the character, the boy,
I identified with most on TV at that time was probably
Davey from *Davey and Goliath,* a Christian stop-motion
animated show produced by the Lutheran Church in
America and Art Clokey, who'd produced the *Gumby*
series, which used the same type of stop-motion anima-

tion, and which I also admired very much. And I felt such a close kinship with Davey because...well...because, I suppose, we were both kids who were motivated chiefly by *metaphysical* concerns. So I was this sort of mystically inclined, spiritually inquisitive little boy with these very secular, very cosmopolitan parents...I was this little boy who was drawn to transubstantiated things...who was always on the lookout for relics, for some occult talismanic object or dusty amulet...with parents who were more into, y'know, more into Scandinavian furniture and hypermodern fondue forks and things like that. That said, I've always recalled my childhood as sublime, as a kind of Eden, as I said. But as I was listening to my mom before—in her wonderful, amazing introduction—it made me begin to remember all sorts of things I guess I'd repressed...I mean, the solitary confinement and sleep deprivation, the force-feeding of beets, the mangled fingers, and the nudity...There's something very *black site* about it all. And so, I hope one of the questions we can begin to address here tonight is: What *was* this childhood? Was it the Garden of Eden or was it Abu Ghraib? Because what begins to emerge here, if all too speculatively, is a whole substratum, a whole buried constellation of petit mal traumas, which orbit around the deepest and the grandest trauma. The death of my first sister registered to me as the loss, the temporary death (in her estranging grief), of my mother. And, of course, loss and abjection are the key motifs in *Gone with the Mind*. And perhaps the ghost of that little sister (the *yūrei*, the *onryō*) is the Imaginary Intern...or the mall shooter...or the disembodied voice of the Reading Group Guide, which can haunt the margins of a person's autobiography like a bad conscience.

When I was ten or so...maybe even younger, maybe eight, nine...I was already thinking to myself: Can a series of completely unrelated, violent, hypersexualized, scatological lines of prose be a kind of writing, a kind of literature? Just one violent, hypersexualized, scatological line of prose after another. *Yama nashi, ochi nashi, imi nashi*—no climax, no resolution, no meaning. Because, I have to say, even then, at eight years of age, every other kind of writing struck me as banal and outdated, and just boring beyond endurance. And I remember very clearly, I must have been in second or third grade, so this would have been about 1964, '65, and I was at some classmate's birthday party at this slot-car racing place...I don't know if you guys even know what slot cars are...I don't even know if they even have slot cars anymore...They were these miniature powered cars that raced around in, uh, little grooves, little slots on a track. And I think this place was in Livingston...or maybe Montclair, I'm not sure. Somewhere in New Jersey. Typical slot-car place, decked out in strobe lights, with all this shiny, polychromatic paraphernalia...And I was standing off by myself, as usual, because I was terribly, terribly shy and extremely introverted, and maladjusted, and basically asocial...but

I remember just being off by myself, mesmerized by the cars whizzing around this track (which must have suggested to me, I realize now in hindsight, a kind of warp-speed synaptic circuitry), just lost in this particular reverie. This is a time in one's life when one only has a very inchoate, wavering sense of one's métier, of course. But even then, at this slot-car raceway in, in...in Livingston, New Jersey—and I can remember this so vividly—thinking of that marvelous phrase coined by the manga artists Sakata Yasuko and Hatsu Akiko: *Yama nashi, ochi nashi, imi nashi,* and realizing that I wanted to do...what?...I didn't know for certain then...but definitely something involving the interlacing of brutality and mysticism. It became obvious to me, at that very moment, amid that delirious hypersynaptic circulation of tiny cars, that my life's work would exhaust itself upon two themes: nerves and nerve—that is, neurology and audacity.

There was a girl in my class, a girl who was not invited to this slot-car party or to *any* parties for that matter, she was pretty much a pariah, in fact...This girl was the first person I ever talked to about things like that. She was the first person—I think Sarah was her name—the first person I felt comfortable enough with, and I suppose kindred enough with, to, even very tentatively, use language like that to try to describe my sensations. Once, we fed each other teaspoonfuls of green Novahistine Elixir, and she said something to me about my bangs that made me feel special...I don't remember exactly what it was, but I remember her auburn hair and her dense freckles and her chapped lips at that moment when she kissed me.

This was a girl who exuberantly chased boys around the schoolyard at recess, boys who were terrified by her webbed fingers, and ran from her in genuine visceral revulsion.

I wonder what's happened to her, I wonder if she's had a decent, happy life, if she's even alive today.

If I were ever asked to give a commencement speech (which I'll *never* be), I'd say basically: They're all gonna laugh at you. Life is pretty much like Carrie's prom. So...stay secret.

The Imaginary Intern and I used to love this commercial for Dove Dry Spray Antiperspirant...There'd be a series of women, and each woman would raise one arm, in a gesture pretty closely resembling the Roman salute, spray on the antiperspirant, stroke her underarm with the index and middle fingers of her other hand, and then snap her fingers to demonstrate that the product "goes on instantly dry." Both of us thought that it was exceptionally beautiful. And if he was watching TV and it came on, and I was doing something somewhere else in the house, he'd call me, he'd call out, "Mark!"...One time he actually called me Tweezers like those kids at summer camp...he was like, "Tweezers! The Dove commercial is on!!" And we started doing the gesture for each other—a quick swipe of the armpit, then a finger snap. It was a cute little thing between us, our little gang sign, I guess. But it's odd...as time went on, it somehow came to mean something much more to us. It came to represent...and this was a completely tacit understanding, not something we ever broached out loud...the gesture came to represent, to symbolize equanimity in the face of death...and perhaps—and I say this in hindsight—perhaps even an infatuation with death.

Once when I came home from school, I opened the front door, and there was my mother at the top of the stairs...as soon as you entered the house, there was a flight of stairs up to the second floor...so I opened the door and there was my mom, standing there completely naked. I think I only glimpsed her for a second, a half a second...because she let out a little yelp of surprise and instantly disappeared into her bedroom. So all I really remember seeing—and it was a shock and a mystery— was that triangle of pubic hair. For the briefest instant. And then her blurred disappearance. But I think the instantaneousness of what I saw contributed to its impact...amplified its subliminal and indelible imprint. In the constructivist juxtaposition of that black triangle against that white oblong there was something spiritual and hieratic, something irreducibly and eternally true, something maybe messianic. (This happened on a Friday afternoon, on the eve of the Sabbath, so it did cross my confused, prepubescent mind, that there might have been some religious significance to it.) Then, that week-end, my parents went to Puerto Rico. I was surprised (shocked, actually) that they just suddenly left for Puerto Rico without having told me that they were even plan-ning on going to Puerto Rico...this wasn't like them at all...So, I assumed that they were going to Puerto Rico (it seemed to me, *fleeing* to Puerto Rico) because I'd seen my mother naked. At that age, correlation almost always implies causation...what's that Latin expression?...*post hoc ergo propter hoc*...after this, therefore because of this.

The naked wraith of my mother flew through time and reappeared at the top of the towering escalator in the Dupont Circle subway station in Washington, DC, on a Friday afternoon ten years later...enchased, like a saint, within the great circular portal of that station. She descended slowly, projecting her fervent gaze into a more distant future, until she was enshrouded in a black blanket, and disappeared in a swarm of braying cops. I remember telling someone once that urologists put such a tremendous amount of Vaseline on their fingers before they do a digital rectal exam that your asshole ends up feeling like an éclair or a cannoli. We have an animal's power of introception—the ability of visceral afferent information to reach awareness...the awareness, for example, of feeling full of Vaseline. But do we have comparable exegetical powers sufficient to understand the symbology of the world outside of our-selves? The world to me has always been a kind of indecipherable cryptogram. For instance, the kids in my bunk at summer camp nicknamed me Tweezers, which, to this day, I simply can't understand...Nor do I understand completely how a naked mother at the top of a flight of stairs and then, ten years later, a naked woman at the top of an escalator...I just don't understand completely how that could happen, or what it means.

I don't know what made me think of this...oh, oh, I actually do know. My mom and I got here a little early tonight, so I went over to the, uh...the Foot Locker, just to look around, kill time...and you know how they have all the different sections for the different kinds of sneakers, like a running section, a basketball section, etc.... So I saw this sign for cross-training sneakers, and that's what made me think of this...I don't know if you guys have ever run into people who do this cute sort of thing when you're talking to them, where if you say, "XYZ," they'll say, "*You're* XYZ"...I knew this girl who used to do it *all* the time...like I'd say something like "There's a hegemonic imperative in cross-training," and she'd say, "*You're* a hegemonic imperative in cross-training." Or we'd be out at a restaurant, and I'd say, "That pasta looks like a bowl of infant foreskins," and she'd say, "*You're* a bowl of infant foreskins." So once, the Imaginary Intern said to me— and I don't remember what the context was—but he said that "memory (and, in a sense, autobiography) is like a rash that blossoms and fades," and I said to him,

"*You're* like a rash that blossoms and fades." And then, after he was gone, I realized that he actually was like a rash that had blossomed and faded...an ache that time won't assuage.

Ever since I was a little boy, I've been trying to reconcile constructivist aesthetics and fascist metaphysics...lucidity and violence...and the endless implications of that dichotomy.

So before I get started tonight, I want to apologize in advance for subjecting you guys to all the ridiculous gesticulations when I read...I have this whole set of ridiculous demagogic tics. And believe me, I wish I didn't, but they're completely involuntary—the clenched fists, the pugnacious outthrust chin and crossed arms, then the clasped hands and heavenward gaze, and, worst of all, the shuckling and the pantomimed mah-jongg shuffling...

Like the preening narcissism of so many physically repulsive men, nothing matches the overweening, magisterial pride of the abject failure, the son manqué. Freud said: "A man who has been the indisputable favorite of his mother keeps for life the feeling of a conqueror." And I believe this remains especially true for the son who has clearly demonstrated that he's capable of accomplishing absolutely nothing.

*   *   *

You lie in bed staring up into the blackness of the room, or into the depths behind your impervious eyelids, and you see a gleam... and at first you mistake it for everything but what it actually is... you mistake it for a segment of the sun's circumference during an annular eclipse, for some diacritical mark, some silver tilde... for, for the wet sex organ of a woman... but it's the gleaming blade of a guillotine, *your* guillotine, your own, special, *bespoke* guillotine poised precariously up there... well, wait, wait... let me try putting it another way... It's either the first thing you've ever seen, which is your mother's shimmering benevolent smile, or the last thing, which is your guillotine. And I think... I was actually thinking about this in the car on the way here tonight... I think what *illumination* really is is when you realize that they're the same thing— that shimmering smile and that gleaming guillotine— they're the same swinging door.

(MARK looks over at the PANDA EXPRESS WORKER. He swipes his armpit with two fingers, then snaps. And with an unexpectedly empathic warmth—)

MARK

Do you see what I mean? They're the same thing.

(The sound of rain hitting the skylight above the food court seems to be getting louder.)

MARK

Okay...before I, uh...get started here, just a couple of little things to help put the excerpts I'm going to read in some context for you...

The Fighter Jets was a cycle of crayon-on-coloring-book and crayon-on-construction-paper works that I produced from roughly 1962 to 1964, which clearly prefigured the violent poetry I would begin writing in 1967, when I was eleven. I was primarily doing...I don't know what you'd call it, I don't know what you'd call the style...*naive* or *primitive* or maybe *outsider, proto-pop* renditions of the U.S. Navy's F4F-3 Wildcat, the Luftwaffe's Messerschmitt Bf 109, and the Imperial Japanese Navy's Mitsubishi A6M Zero...these three fighter aircraft were...these were my water lilies, I guess you could say. One could arrange the work in three loose thematic clusters: fighter jets in flight either singly or in formation, aerial battles or dogfights between fighter jets featuring multicolored tracer ammunition fired from mounted 20 mm autocannons, and in which one or both of the fighter aircraft are in flames and/or exploding in the air, and (in a series I completed in late '64) kamikaze fighters smashing their jets into American battleships and aircraft carriers.

This latter series foreshadows one of the first poems that I submitted to a poetry workshop at Brandeis University when I was a freshman there in 1973, which was the first actual writing class I ever took. My classmates were all seniors, all several years older than me, very dour and humorless, and very cliquish and condescending toward me, and I wanted nothing more than for them to respect me and include me, and I guess my way of trying to ingratiate myself with them, of just trying to get them to like me—which I so *desperately* wanted—was to hand in increasingly aggressive, abrasive poems with disassociated imagery, jarring, dissonant non sequiturs, and increasingly antagonistic titles, basically an update of my proprietary vernacular of *yama nashi, ochi nashi, imi nashi* that I'd intuited years ago at the slot-car track in Livingston. So this poem I was referring to, for instance, had two stanzas; the first was...and I can't remember the exact words, obviously...but it was something like: "Asked to describe the rabbi's daughters, / the man doffs his baseball cap, / revealing the sunspotted flesh of his balding head, / and pauses for a moment... / 'The second daughter is more beautiful than the first, the third more beautiful than the second, and the first more beautiful than the third.'" And then the second stanza which was quite, quite long—it ran fifteen or twenty-some-odd pages—was intended as the dying soliloquy, the...the soliloquy in extremis, of a plummeting kamikaze pilot, except that you couldn't possibly know that it was a dying soliloquy or any other kind of soliloquy for that matter, because it was written entirely as a spurious transliteration of completely fake Japanese, nor could you possibly know that it involved a kamikaze pilot, because although I'd originally entitled the poem "Kamikaze," on the morning of the workshop, at the very last minute, I changed the title to "Eat Me. I Hate Everyone in This Fucking Class," probably as a kind of preemptive provocation, assuming that the class would hate the poem (which the class vehemently did). And when people predictably took offense at the title, I remember explaining that "Well...it's not me who's actually saying that, it's the narrator of the poem, it's a character I'm playing," that sort of thing. And of course I read my poem out loud, which is what we did in the workshop, and I read the faux-Japanese gibberish section in its entirety, which, seriously, must have taken about forty minutes, and which I could see just completely aggravated the shit out of everyone in the class. And all I really wanted out of all this was for someone, one of my peers, to just say to me, *Look, I really appreciate how hard you're working* or *I really appreciate how much you're trying to do something unique or transformative or just fresh, something we haven't heard before, or at least trying to wring some droll human comedy from the unrelenting grimness and abject indignity of life on this planet.* But no one did. But, remarkably, Mark Strand, who was a very well-known, highly esteemed poet, who died fairly recently, and who was teaching this workshop back then...he actually seemed to *get* it. He said to the class—and, again, I'm paraphrasing something that was said a very long time ago—he said that the first part represented the enchantment and illogic and fear and suspense of beauty, and that all the ensuing faux-Japanese gibberish represented the incommunicable subjective reality of experiencing that beauty. So, surprised—shocked, actually—and sort of emboldened by what certainly seemed like Strand's genuine engagement with the work, I piped up (and I was usually too bashful to say *anything*) and I said, somewhat flippantly and presumably to lighten the mood a bit, "I'm trying to do the Baal Shem Tov with a *Tora! Tora! Tora!* vibe," but then I thought to myself, *You know what, I am going to make a case for this poem, and I am going to explain exactly what I did and why.* I was a great admirer of Andy Warhol then (and still am), and I got such a kick out of his coyness and his diffidence and nonchalance when he'd be asked why he silkscreened his paintings or why he'd just point his stationary 16 mm Bolex at a building or a fellated or sleeping man and let it run until the emulsion flickered and whitened and the cartridge expired, and this pale, pimply sphinx in his sunglasses would put his finger on his chin and think for a moment or two, and then just say, "Because it was easier." But I wasn't like that at all. As much as I would have liked to have been a pale and pimply sphinx, I had an uncommonly clear complexion and I had a decidedly unsphinxlike need for people to understand what I was doing and to admire it and to like me. And I certainly hadn't done what I did because it was easier—it was extraordinarily time-consuming and laborious and difficult to write that amount of faux-Japanese gibberish because real words kept inadvertently popping up in the gibberish. And I explained how it's almost impossible to completely purge a text of meaning.

Meaning is like mice or eczema—it's very hard, if not impossible, to get rid of completely. Not only because the purging itself, like a dance, or like a new science, generates a whole new signifying language of its own, but because meaning persists at much deeper levels than we can ever imagine and at a much more infinitesimal scale, gigantic monsters can be created by changing a single nucleotide in the genetic code—one can conjure an ornate, vanished world from outer space from the serif of a single letter. What else does the human being do but emit and decipher signs? Who else but the human being has this compulsion for finding patterns and structures in all sorts of incoherent noise (and craquelure!). With gibberish, you open the floodgates of meaning, everything is in there—actual poems by Saigyō and Fujiwara no Teika and Princess Shikishi (if that's what you're looking for), mitochondrial DNA sequences from honeybees and ants and aphids, blocks of AES/Rijndael-256–encrypted ciphertext, backwards excerpts from *Don Quixote* and *Little Dorrit,* from Gwyneth Paltrow's *It's All Good: Delicious, Easy Recipes That Will Make You Look Good and Feel Great,* long diagonal acrostics of John Galliano's anti-Semitic tirade at La Perle bar in Le Marais... everything. In the faux-Japanese glossolalia of the plummeting kamikaze is the complete anagram of *Gone with the Mind* that would take scientists (i.e., the Imaginary Intern and myself) another forty years to unscramble. His gibberish is the incommunicable anguish that results from the impossibility of fulfilling incestual desire. He is, like a muttering

Popeye, a hysteric describing his symptoms, destroying the world in order to save it. The vertiginous illogic, the impossibility of the exorbitant claims about the beauty of the rabbi's daughters causes nausea. A little boy is having a tantrum because his mother is impossibly gone. He vomits gibberish. In the distance is a kamikaze's long parabolic swoon. A little boy's tantrum crescendos in a parabolic projection of vomited gibberish which is actually a secret language between kamikaze boy and the rabbi's daughter who represents—drumroll, please—the mother!

I don't know how long I went on like this. It was like a fugue state...as if I were back in my bedroom in Jersey City holding forth for my orangutan and my Civil War soldiers...and when I "returned" to the classroom in Waltham, all the students had left, only Strand remained. "Y'know," I said to him, "I was originally going to entitle the poem 'Kamikaze,' but I thought that might be a little too on the nose." "Nonsense!" he said, with a snort of laughter. "With the possible exception of 'Eat Me. I Hate Everyone in This Fucking Class,' what else could you possibly call it?!" And then he said—and this is something I remember *so* vividly, something I really appreciated and would ruminate upon for a long time to come—he said, "The explanation of your poem is a better poem than the poem. It's even more insane." He was a charming, congenial, exceptionally sweet person, very generous, very gracious, very receptive and encouraging, with this quick, mischievous sense of humor. Just a really, really good guy. I remember feeling that so much at the time, even though, deep down, I suspected that he was just humoring me, and was probably saying vastly different things at the off-campus coffee klatches that I was always much too shy and insecure to ever attend. But he also knew—and that he knew is something I've surmised in retrospect—that there was something up with me, that there was something going on psychologically. Why else would I insist on entitling poem after poem "Shit in a Ramekin"? "Shit in a Ramekin II," "Shit in a Ramekin III," "Shit in a Ramekin IV," etc. No matter what they were about. I wrote a poem that was just a very standard, sort of elegiac reminiscence about taking a nap on a summer afternoon in Deal, New Jersey, and hearing, through the open window, the sound of lawn mowers and birds singing and children playing, and I called it "Shit in a Ramekin V." Another one I remember was inspired by one of those automated promptings you hear at airports. It went something like:

The moving walkway
Is now ending.
Please look
Down.

This was called "Shit in a Ramekin VI" or "Shit in a Ramekin VII" or something.

*   *   *

I was full of anger back then, but obviously so desperate for people to like me, and so predisposed to loathe anyone who did in fact like me, *that* whole routine...of rapid-cycling neediness and misanthropy...And as arbitrary as it might seem to think of oneself purely in terms of Teds, I think, inside, I was definitely feeling more like Ted Bundy or Ted Kaczynski than Ted Hughes or Ted Berrigan back then.

I have to say that, after all these years, I'm still vain enough to prefer having enemies over friends. It's still consoling to me to feel embattled and anathematized. I'm still grateful for anything that drives me back into my little corner of the world (this is my innate, roach-like thigmotropism), for anything that forces me to seek refuge in my ancestral village...what the Imaginary Intern used to call "Studio Mizuhō" or "Around the Corner Where Fudge Is Made"...the primordial matrix of the mind, the ancestral home of the mind, what the fifteenth-century Noh playwright Komparu Zenchiku called the "circle of emptiness" (*kurin*)—the stage at which the actor transcends distinctions between pure and orthodox styles and improper styles, achieving a return to the beginning (*kyarai*), the highest, indescribable experience, which expresses nothing. And, of course, this is that very place within one's mother's arms, that very circle formed by one's mother's arms. And I still believe that there are two basic kinds of people— people who cultivate the narcissistic delusion of being watched at all times through the viewfinder of a camera, and people who cultivate the paranoid delusion of being watched at all times through the high-powered optics of a sniper's rifle, and I think I fall—and have always fallen—into this latter category.

But the ridiculous thing about being an angry young man, or at least an angry young Brandeis freshman, is that you don't even know yet how much there is out there to actually be angry about. Things are still fairly idyllic at that age. You have no idea yet the extent to which life really is shit in a ramekin.

A week or so later, I had one last meeting with Strand, just the two of us in his office. "Do you know that the band Roxy Music has a song out now called 'Do the Strand'?" I asked him. He seemed genuinely perturbed by this. "What?! I need to contact my attorney immediately!" he said, waiting for my distress to register before cracking up. He really could be such a funny guy. I told him I wanted to quit the class, and he said, "I don't blame you." I felt so relieved, so "safe" at that moment, that I confessed to him my lifelong love of Mickey Mantle and Jackie Gleason. And I remember I started to cough, and Strand asked me if I was okay, and I said, "I've been choking on the same stupid piece of barley since lunch," and he opened a small bottle of Pellegrino for me, and…no…I'm sorry…I'm sorry…my God, they're going to confiscate my Nonfiction at the Food Court membership card here…it was Orangina, not Pellegrino…one of those little ten-ounce bottles of Orangina... So, I took a couple of sips, which helped a lot... and I, uh, don't remember how we got around to the subject of Popeye, maybe it was via Ashbery's sestina "Farm Implements and Rutabagas in a Landscape." And I'm not sure if I actually mentioned this to Strand at the time or not, but I think when most people visualize Popeye, the first thing that probably comes to mind is his can of magic spinach (which made him, for all intents and purposes, the first celebrity user of performance-enhancing drugs), or the battleships and the turbines and the atomic bombs superimposed on his swollen biceps, or his cri de guerre "I yam what I yam, and that's all what I yam," which, in its concision, transparency, and tautological plenitude, remains the first and greatest constructivist autobiography; but he also had a very beautiful way of speaking, particularly of speaking to himself—his muttering. It was this streaming, autobiographical play-by-play overlaid with all sorts of commentary and theorizing, this meta-mutter, the soliloquy of an electrolarynx, a sort of free-jazz didgeridoo solo. It's kind of like what Strand had said to me the previous week in class, about how the explanation of my poem was a better poem than the poem. I think Popeye's muttering is the explanation of *his* poem. (This is very similar to something the Imaginary Intern and I used to call "singing all the parts." If you ask someone—and I'm just picking a song I happened to hear on the radio in the car on the way over here tonight—"Do you like that Michael Jackson song 'Black and White'?" and she's like, "I don't know it, how's it go?" you'd try to do the song for her, to re-create it for her. You'd try to approximate some of the percussion with your mouth, to whatever extent you could do that, a little bit of beat-boxing…and then you'd lay in that guitar riff…De-de-de-de-de-duuh, de-de-de-duuh…De-de-de-de-de-duuh, de-de-de-duuh…High-pitched yelp…De-de-de-de-de-duuh, de-de-de-duuh…De-de-de-de-de-duuh, de-de-de-duuh…High-pitched yelp…"I took my baby on a Saturday bang / Boy is that girl with you / Yes we're one and the same…" That's "singing all the parts." In the actual song, it's all layered, like a pastry, like a…like a mille-feuille…a napoleon. But when you're just doing it by yourself, you have to take all of it apart…it becomes more like an Ikea exploded diagram…and what's simul-taneous, what's synchronic in the music, becomes sort of flattened out and sequential in the representation. And this was something the Imaginary Intern and I used to al-ways talk about trying to do in *Gone with the Mind,* trying somehow to express the chord of how one feels at a single given moment, in this transient, phantom world, standing in the center of a food court at a mall with your mom, but in the arpeggiated exploded diagram of an autobiogra-phy.) So then, Strand asked if I'd liked comics when I was a kid, and I said that Popeye was a relatively recent inter-est, but that, yes, when I was a little boy there were comics I liked very much. "Which ones?" he said. "I'm curious." And I remember he was rotating his wrist as if he might have hurt it sailing or playing tennis. And I explained to him that most boys I knew who were into comics at that age were, y'know, either into Marvel, things like Spider-Man, Iron Man, the Hulk, Thor, X-Men, or into DC, stuff like Superman and Batman and Green Lantern. But somehow I got steered into Harvey Comics, and Harvey Comics...their roster of "heroes" consisted of an assortment of, uh...of, basically, pathetic, feckless, feeble-minded pariahs. (These were, come to think of it, actually the first misfits I "befriended.") A couple of them were clearly psychotic, but, for the most part, they were just fantastically stupid—I mean like mentally defective, low-grade-moron stupid...a bunch of guffawing, gullible half-wits who just wanted everyone to be their friend, who'd get into a car with anyone, sell their souls for a cupcake literally made out of crap, follow a fucking balloon off the ledge of a building...But I just found myself identifying with them in a particularly intense way. I felt that they related uncannily to everything I was going through in my life at that time, and I guess I also thought, even at that age, that they were, in some sense, the most poetic of all the comic-book characters—Sad Sack, the luckless, disaffected, humiliated soldier; Baby Huey, the ungainly, naive, dimwitted, friendless, anthropomorphic duck; Little Lotta, a homely, obese girl whose insatiable gluttony gave her superhuman strength which she'd use to help people who still found her completely revolting; Hot Stuff, a devil-baby who wore asbestos diapers; and, of course, Casper, the friendly, cloyingly obsequious ghost...I just really connected, on a very deep level, with these characters. And the question is: What was it inside me, what gnawing void or strangulated loop of psyche had produced such a strong feeling of fellowship with a lonely, anomic army private with latent spree-killing tendencies, a retarded duck, a bullied fat girl, an incontinent demon, and a desperately ingratiating dead child? And I think the answer has to be, for reasons that are all too apparent, my PTSD from being force-fed beets, from being abandoned on an out-of-control merry-go-round operated by some depraved drifter, the brutality, the inhumanity of the Ferbering, having my fingers deliberately mangled in a carpet cleaner, being left in a filthy, stinking, cacophonous, violent hospital ward all by myself after a tonsillectomy that I'm pretty sure was performed without anesthesia... and also from just having to watch my mom vomit and hemorrhage all over the place —

(MARK winks at his MOM, who's shaking her head, smiling with forbearance.)

MARK

So, Strand looked at me, and he said, "You should write about all this someday." And I said, "You mean about all the terrible privations and wrenching traumas from my childhood?" And he said, "Yes, it would be hilarious!" And I said, "You mean... nonfiction?"

And, well, here we are... some forty years later... at the Nonfiction at the Food Court Reading Series.

Tonight, taking refuge from the metaphysical nausea and dislocation *out there,* we consecrate this food court in the name of nonfiction; tonight we exalt and exult in the Credible, *in here.* And, before I get started here, I'd just like to second my mom's words of gratitude for Jenny Schoenhals, the senior general manager at Woodcreek Plaza Mall, who, as my mom said, worked so diligently and without whom none of this would be possible. I don't know if it has anything to do with the heavy rain or the flash-flood warnings or the possibility of mall shooters or what, but I'm sorry she couldn't be here tonight. And, uh...you know something? If, perhaps—and I'm just thinking out loud here—Jenny Schoenhals is not here tonight because she's become disillusioned by the material world and renounced it, including her family and her profession, and she's taken a vow of silence and itinerant solitude, and set out to walk across the country barefoot, living off alms, chanting and praying...if she's shaved her head and wears a mask over her mouth to avoid inadvertently ingesting insects...if she's chosen to do that, then I say, Right on, Jenny. You fuckin' go, girl. If she's abjured the food court in her anorexia mirabilis, then I say, Bravo, bravissimo! And I dedicate this reading to you. You strike a heavy blow, martyr, in your death fast, and we hope that the glow of your starving, autophagic body signals the serrated nano-UFOs to descend from space and tunnel into the aortas and urethras of all the terrible men who've turned me down for jobs my whole life...these men I've had to pander to, to try and ingratiate myself with over all these years...All you hitherto imaginary, sausage-shaped, GPS-guided, sodomizing necrodrones—by the power of Satan I command you!—hurtle down from outer space and bury yourselves in the assholes of all the men who've made me grovel for crumbs and work for scale. These are the same kinds of men that my mom so eloquently denounced in her introduction...so condescending...so dismissive and smug...My mom swore at them. Remember? Remember when she was describing how she reviled them, how she spat at them when they returned in their fishing boats...in their ships?!

Now hold on...hold on...

(MARK motions for quiet as if to quell a stir his remarks have provoked, which they have not.)

MARK

We're all adults here—we all know the score. We know what they do to people like me and my mom, to paradoxical hybrids of arrogant narcissism and vulnerable naïveté. We know what happens to unreconstructed surrealist militants. Tortured. Marked for assassination. Imagine what awaits me out there.

In the thrall of biological determinism and acculturation, we're left very little wiggle room.

We now know (and didn't back then in 1973, when Strand and I sat in his office, casually discussing sestinas and ekphrasis) that genetic variations in brain morphology, weight, age, diet, alcohol, drug, and tobacco use, toxic exposure, exercise routines, etc., have more to do with a writer's style than the comics he read when he was young.

In 1955, the year my mom was pregnant with me, Bertolt Brecht voted Mao Zedong's essay "On Contradiction" the "best book" he had read in the past twelve months, a period of time that saw the publication of William Golding's *Lord of the Flies,* Kingsley Amis's *Lucky Jim,* Sloan Wilson's *The Man in the Gray Flannel Suit,* J.R.R. Tolkien's *The Lord of the Rings,* and Dr. Seuss's *Horton Hears a Who!* Mao...a guy who never brushed his teeth, who just rinsed his mouth out with tea when he woke up...who, according to his personal physician, Li Zhisui, never cleaned his genitals. Instead, Mao said, "I wash myself inside the bodies of my women." The Imaginary Intern and I were great admirers of Mao's *Talks at the Yan'an Forum on Literature and Art* and we diligently tried to apply his dictum "Discard what is backward and develop what is revolutionary" to the production of *Gone with the Mind,* and although I agree with Mao that one should bathe infrequently, and that when one does, one should use the vaginal flora of other creatures instead of soap, I subscribe unswervingly to the conviction that a gentleman should never go out in public at night without pomaded hair and heavy cologne...

(MARK cocks his head to one side, as if he hears, in the sudden cascade of hail against the skylight, the siren song of death itself.)

MARK

In hindsight, I think probably the most significant thing about *The Fighter Jets* cycle is how the multicolor gunfire spewing from the fighter jets in those early crayon drawings resembled a kind of weaponized vomit, obviously an allusion to my mom's hyperemesis gravidarum (which she'd eventually sublimate into her logorrhea), and also—and this is another of those things that just occurred to me in the car on the way here tonight— how those fighter jets so clearly presage the motif of Mussolini's flying balcony in *Gone with the Mind.*

Now, *The Bethesda Blow Jobs* were a series of blow jobs I received in the late seventies, in a car parked in a lot outside a large office complex in Rockville, Maryland (why my mom and I came to refer to them as *The Bethesda Blow Jobs*, I really can't say). The person giving me the blow jobs was a woman who was my boss, my supervisor, at the time. And she was a particularly intelligent, very precise, very punctilious kind of person, actually a very imposing person, and I remember thinking at the time that here was a sort of grande dame in the making. This basically all came about because I shared a tiny little office with this very nebbishy, sallow, stoop-shouldered middle-aged guy, whose name I can't remember at the moment. This was a documentanalysis company that was used primarily by law firms involved in very complex litigation like huge class-action suits, for instance, where'd there'd be massive amounts of documentation like reports and memoranda and correspondence and interviews and interrogatories that all needed to be collated and synopsized and classified or coded. So anyway, this unfortunate guy I shared the office with was just an especially unprepossessing, awkward and excruciatingly goofy, completely uncool person who was effectively shunned by everyone and who didn't have a single friend, a single person to even talk to in the entire office. And I think he'd just undergone some pretty serious gastrointestinal surgery because after lunch his stomach would start rumbling, I mean *seriously* rumbling...he'd get this, y'know...what's the medical term?...this, uh...this *borborygmus*...he'd get this borborygmus like I'd never heard in my life, it was like the shifting of tectonic plates or something...and then there'd be this whistling sound, this high-pitched sibilance, like there was some kind of pressurized internal leak in there...and then he'd fall dead asleep sitting in his chair...for quite a while...for, like, an hour, an hour and a half. And for whatever reason—I honestly can't say—I developed this keen affection for him. He was actually the only person in that entire office that I felt at all comfortable with. I really felt a genuine kindredness with him. And when he'd fall asleep, I'd code his quota of documents for him, and I remember thinking one afternoon, as he was snoring and drooling on himself at his desk, that maybe this was my act of atonement for having swindled all the bright Crayolas from that color-blind boy back in second grade at James F. Murray No. 38 Elementary School. Anyway, late one afternoon, as I was about to head home, my boss—*our* boss—pulled me aside and said that she was attracted to me because I'd "befriended a misfit," to use her exact words, which I thought sounded like something out of one of those fantasy novels, like I'd "betrothed a gnome" or something. And she told me that I deserved a merit badge for it…which was such a particularly funny, particularly uncanny thing for her to have said, because when I was about eight years old and I was a Cub Scout, all the boys in our den were sitting around in the kitchen of our den mother one afternoon, and she lit a cigarette bending over the flame from the front burner on the stove, and she set her hair on fire, and I put it out—I don't remember if I just smothered it with my hands or doused it with some Sprite or what— but she stared at me with this sort of demented look of gratitude on her face (she drank) and she said, "I'm going to recommend that you get a merit badge for this," and sure enough I did, I actually got a merit badge for extinguishing the fire in our den mother's hair. So, back to Bethesda—I'm sorry, *Rockville*—and *that* merit badge. Just about every afternoon—and this went on for a couple of months, I think—my boss and I would stroll to her car after work, and she'd sit in the driver's seat and I'd sit in the passenger seat and she'd unbuckle my belt, and...it was all very rote...she would always say—each and every single time—"Let me expedite that" when I'd start to fumble with the buttons on her blouse, and she never failed to remind me that she was attracted to me not because of how I looked (although she'd always interject that I was "more than adequate in that regard"), but because of how alluring she thought it was that I'd, y'know, "befriended a misfit." And I remember being extremely impressed that even in these encounters, which I suppose were a bit risqué at the time, she maintained the hierarchical tenor of our relationship by using words like *expedite* and *in that regard*. And so there I'd sit, in that passenger seat (she was obviously so much the pilot of this particular flying balcony), and I'd just gaze vacantly out the window at the procession, at the cavalcade of exhausted, bedraggled, bleary-eyed people who'd just spent the last eight hours coding documents, making their quota, and were plodding like zombies to their cars, and I'd meekly wave good-bye to any of them who happened to make eye contact with me. And I should mention that this woman—my boss—has since become an extraordinarily successful, high-powered, and internationally influential CEO, someone akin to, say, Meg Whitman at Hewlett-Packard or Marillyn Hewson at Lockheed Martin. And I mention this primarily because chronic financial insecurity and improvidence and the sense of ever teetering on the precipice of catastrophic failure are such integral motifs in *Gone with the Mind*—the fifty-eight-year-old son who still needs to borrow money from his mother, who still depends on his mother for rides to the mall, etc., etc. And this is a...a situation, a dilemma that is getting worse, more intractable for me as I get older, and I really can't see any solution to it on the horizon at this point in my life. I've never really had anything even remotely resembling a feasible financial strategy, with the possible exception of a very inchoate plan that involved trying to arrange a marriage between my daughter and the television host and producer Ryan Seacrest, a marriage which one can only imagine would make things considerably easier financially for me, and even this plan, I'm pretty sure, was the Imaginary Intern's idea which he dubbed Operation Seacrest and which never really progressed much beyond the planning stages, although the sobriquet almost immediately became the code name for any moneymaking scheme, however penny ante, and then very quickly became the code name for just about *anything* we might be doing. So if I was going to, I don't know, make a peanut butter and jelly sandwich, or...or eat a package of Peeps, or go work out at the gym or just do a couple of sets of Kegel exercises up in the attic, or, y'know, just take a shower or do some laundry—any of that would qualify as Operation Seacrest. And, of course, if we were feeling the least bit paranoid and that we needed to be especially clandestine, or you know something, just because we felt like it, just because, I don't know, it was Friday and we were feeling a little reckless and crazy, we'd refer to the autobiography itself as Operation Seacrest or maybe even just OpCrest. The only thing that we would never *ever* even think of referring to as Operation Seacrest was the Soviet defense of Stalingrad during the Second World War, a topic that was—and I'm pretty sure I mentioned this before—a topic that was completely sacrosanct.

Kingsley Amis once said that religion and masturbation were alike in one regard: feel free to practice them, but no one really wants to hear you go on about it. Which I just think is completely wrong. I mean, I just couldn't disagree with that statement more vehemently. I think religion and masturbation are probably the two most interesting things a person could *ever* talk about. And you'll be able to, make your own assessment once you've actually heard the excerpts, but I think a very strong case could be made that *Gone with the Mind* is fundamentally an autobiography *of* religion and masturbation, that is to say, an ontogenetic history of religion and masturbation, a study of religion and masturbation as it pertains to an individual organism, an individual organism whose first erection was inspired by a viewing of Carl Dreyer's 1928 silent film *The Passion of Joan of Arc*, which was shown to us by our seventh-grade English teacher, a bulimic ex-nun who, as it turned out, was *very* fond of my poetry. This, of course, predates by a good six months or so the dawning of my erotic obsession with Nadezhda Chizhova, a twenty-two-year-old Soviet shot-putter, whose photograph I first beheld in an old issue of *Life* magazine, which I'd unearthed one summer at a house in Deal, New Jersey, that my parents co-owned with my grandparents (my mom's parents, Raymond and Harriet) and my uncle and aunt (Lew and Fran, my mom's sister), and which, like all shore houses, boasted an extensive archive of moldering magazines that any pubescent boy with a lot of time on his hands (free time being surely the greatest gift that summer bestows on a pubescent boy) can scour for prurient images, which in my case could be simply a sweaty, androgenized Eastern European woman flinging a discus or putting a shot.

In retrospect, I can see that it was my incipient questioning of the unified subject and of normative meaning (as well as the onset of puberty) that led me from Sad Sack and Baby Huey to Mickey Mantle to these autoerotic assignations with Nadezhda Chizhova. And soon I'd feel as if I'd betrayed Nadezhda, I really did...I think we're much more chivalrous when we're young than when we get older...because I also started leering at photographs of her great rivals, the two East German shot-putters Margitta Gummel and Ilona Slupianek, both of whom were given Oral-Turinabol, the androgenic anabolic steroid used by the East German government in its State Plan 14.25 under the supervision of Stasi, the GDR state secret police. (I really think it helped me immeasurably to relate to other people when I realized that we all probably remember, with an especially fine-grained attention to detail, the first time we masturbated to pictures of a doped athlete.) This was a period of time when I began associating photographs of androgenized Eastern European women throwing javelins and tossing hammers with my own gratification. For me, the steroids they took bestowed an aura of martyrdom upon them. The Oral-Turinabol seemed to endow them with an excess or superfluity of sexuality, an excrescence of sexuality...a burden, which I found tremendously arousing...I was beginning to realize that sexuality (the drives, the impulses, the appendages themselves) is a kind of cross to bear, a heavy shackle one's obligated to drag around...and the heavier and more cumbersome, the sexier—if that makes any sense. It was also a time when I began to view my own penis as an instrument of self-annihilation. As a "way out" for my mind.

It is evidence of my own curatorial slackness that I neglected to save these images of Chizhova, Gummel, and Slupianek, which, over time, had actually bleached in the feral, polymorphous intensity of my...my *scopophilic* gaze.

I should add that, for me, there was an aura of martyrdom about Mickey Mantle too, with his fractured kneecap, his torn ACL, the cartilage damage, the osteomyelitis and cirrhosis and hepatitis...the photographs of Mantle applying thick wraps to both of his knees before each and every game, and then soaking in a stainless-steel whirlpool bath after each game...And, of course, I ogled those photographs as one might ogle paintings of Saint Sebastian bound to a stake and impaled with arrows. I had a treasured issue of *Life* magazine (July 30, 1965) with a cover story about Mickey Mantle entitled "Mantle's Misery." The subhead was "He Faces Physical Pain and a Fading Career." And because I strove to emulate Mantle so absolutely, I very much desired similar physical pain and, even as a little boy, very much aspired to a fading career. I think I took care of the first part when, in the assassination attempt my mom mentioned in her introduction, I was hit by a car in Culver City, California, and tore the meniscus, anterior cruciate ligament, and medial collateral ligament in my left knee, almost identical injuries to those Mantle sustained when he tripped over an exposed drainpipe in center field during the second game of the 1951 World Series against the Giants. And as far as the second part goes, the "fading career," if tonight's turnout is any indication, I've succeeded in that regard beyond my wildest expectations.

As a child, I was a huge, obsessive Yankees fan. And I remember, especially when we were at that summerhouse in Deal, that house on Neptune Avenue...I could only stay up until about the fifth inning, so my mom would listen to the rest of the game on the radio, the whole game, even if it went into extra innings, and then in the morning, as soon as she woke up and came downstairs for breakfast (I'd have been up for hours waiting impatiently, listening for her instantly recognizable footsteps on the creaky stairs), she'd narrate those last innings for me, pitch by pitch, play by play...with all her Proustian divagations and endlessly ramifying digressions, tangents splitting off into other tangents...with all her allusion and analogies...the bad hop of a ground ball to Bobby Richardson or Tony Kubek or maybe Joe Pepitone conjuring up the story of a second cousin who was hit in the forehead by a stone expelled by a power mower, causing a gash that required plastic surgery which was, of course, botched by an incompetent doctor, resulting in an endless lawsuit (medical malpractice being a favorite subject of my mom and myself). An inning could easily take an hour. My mom has formidable, world-class raconteurial skills. She really does. She's a consummate, virtuosic storyteller. The fastidious descriptions, the lavish scene-setting, perfectly punctured by some choice vulgarity or solecism...the vivid, impeccably pitched portrayals of disparate characters, the timing, the accents and intonations, the shifting registers of body language...she can make a trip to the dry cleaner seem like *The Ring of the Nibelung.* And because my mother is such a good and loving person, a woman of such unparalleled magnanimity, these stories were never ultimately disparaging or censorious, however heinous the protagonist's behavior had been. There was always some redemptive concluding note, some flourish of sympathy and approbation. Whether the person had deliberately drowned her own dog or fucked her dying husband's oncologist, my mom would somehow find a way to append some sort of favorable coda to it all. "The woman's become the most devoted grandmother I've ever seen," she'll remark. "My God, how she dotes on those grandkids with the Ice Capades and the *Nutcracker* tickets and the PoshTots ball gowns, the uh...the Petit Bateau rain slickers, those adorable little fuchsia Stella McCartney bomber jackets...She spends a fortune on those kids!"

And would these kids even care that their grandmother carried on with their late grandfather's doctor in his office at Sloan Kettering a couple of times a week? I seriously doubt it. *Good for her!* they'd probably say. *We love Grandma. She takes us to all kinds of cool places and buys us all kinds of cool stuff. She can fuck whomever she wants to...Grandpa didn't really do shit with us. He always seemed too busy and preoccupied with work...or too sick.*

When you're a child, you're just doing everything intuitively, you're just using what the Imaginary Intern and I used to call Inuit Intuition (we both loved all things *Arctic*)...you're just joyriding with your id at the wheel, thrashing around in a continuous tumult of what South Korean director Kim Jee-woon calls "the good, the bad, and the weird"...which is what life is back then...you're just acting (I don't mean in the sense of theater, although that too), you're just doing things, committing random deeds...And it's only much later in life that we try to retrospectively map out, to plot all the traumas and the triumphs, the lucky breaks and lost opportunities, all the decisions and their ramifying consequences. And I tend to believe that this inclination to look back on one's life and superimpose a teleological narrative of cause and effect is probably itself a symptom of incipient dementia, caused by some prion disease or the clumping of beta-amyloid plaques. Certainly as we get older, we begin to compulsively revise, re-edit, and rearrange—like screenwriters thumbtacking index cards to a bulletin board—the same finite repertoire of autobiographical scenes in our memory to see if perhaps the latest rehash might provide any new answers to those fundamental and persistently intractable questions like: How the fuck did this all happen? How the fuck did things ever get to this point? How the fuck did I end up becoming the person I am now? Especially, this...this particularly baroque, *grotesque* version of the person I am now? To properly answer questions like these would probably require a prolonged period of masochistic self-absorption. But I suppose, in a way, that's why we're all here tonight...Am I right, folks?

(PANDA EXPRESS WORKER and SBARRO WORKER remain oblivious, one bobbing his head to something he's listening to on his headphones, the other watching a Snapchat on his cell phone of his girlfriend making fart bubbles in a bathtub.)

MARK

Jeffrey Hammerbacher, a professor of genetics and genomic sciences at the Icahn School of Medicine at Mount Sinai, wrote something very interesting when he was seven years old. He wrote, *My favorite hobby is doing*

*math while I'm eating. I like doing this because math is my favorite
subject and I like to eat.*

Well, doing *this* is *my* favorite subject, and I like to eat
too. So it's extremely gratifying to be here tonight, reading *Gone with the Mind* at the food court.

I think I mentioned before that the Imaginary Intern
sometimes functioned like a . . . like a kind of trainer for
me. So before we started actually working on the autobiography, for about the first three months, he just
had me playing video games and eating cookie dough.
And then one night he posted a winky face on my Face-
book, and it was like "Game on." And the first thing
we started working on, which was completely out of
sequence, was something that happened back in my senior year at Brandeis. My dad had called and told me
that Eli—a second cousin of mine, whom I didn't really
know particularly well—was going to . . . to Tufts, I think
it was . . . starting at Tufts as a freshman . . . and that it
would be nice if I visited him. Eli also wanted to be a
writer, according to my dad, and we might have a lot to
talk about, and it would just be a nice thing to do. So, I
go to visit this guy in his dorm room at Tufts, and we're
drinking some beer and talking about this and that, and
at some point he excuses himself to go to the bathroom,
and he's in there for a while, so I'm snooping around
his room, checking out his books, rifling through his al-
bums, and I find, on his desk, a draft of a short story he's
working on, this very, very short, Lydia Davis–length
story, and I read it, and . . . obviously I can't remember

the story, this was almost forty years ago...but I distinctly remember its tenor, which I can try to give you at least some flavor of...I mean, I'm just making this up off the top of my head to try to convey the tone...

When the Red Army breached the German front in 1945, Nazi propaganda minister Don Draper would try to lighten the mood in the bunker by fucking a microwaved Bacon Cheddar Hot Pocket.

(The PANDA EXPRESS WORKER actually looks up for a moment here.)

MARK

Something like that...Anyway, this guy Eli comes back from the bathroom, and he catches me reading it, which he's perfectly cool with, and he says, "Y'know, that's just the first draft, would you like to read the second draft?" And I said, "Yes, sure." And here's the interesting part of the story—there was a total, bewildering discrepancy between the first draft and the second draft which was this unfailingly decorous, almost Chekhovian twenty-five-page story about an aging spinster who sang Schubert lieder in her attic, a handsome young parson with a humiliating stutter, a pair of Yorkshire terriers, and an heirloom cupboard. So I said to him—and, in retrospect, probably should have just kept my mouth shut—that I preferred the first draft (which I genuinely did; yes, the second draft was very sad in that artisanal way that makes a certain kind of sophisticated reader very happy, and yes, the first draft was a bit adolescent and unrepentantly stupid—sometimes stupidity is the only "way out" for the mind—but it had a certain flip brio to it that I appreciated a lot, and from which I took no small degree of inspiration). And this just really baffled Eli, really perplexed him. And we ended up talking about it for the rest of the night...I think we went out for burgers and shots and beer somewhere in the neighborhood and had this long, very congenial, super-earnest-undergrad kind of debate about the relative merits of draft one and draft two and how they might be analogous to certain sociopolitical currents, etc. And I remember saying...we'd left the bar and were out on the street somewhere...and I was *so* wasted...I was swaying back and forth...I had to grab onto a...a...telephone pole to stay upright...and I remember saying: "If we've learned anything from Lévi-Strauss, it's that individual motifs mean nothing in any abstract sense until they are placed in a structural relationship with other motifs." And then I passed out. And I don't remember anything else from that night...Actually the whole rest of that senior year is a kind of blur after that. And then years later, my dad calls me one night and he says, "Do you remember your cousin Eli?" And I go, "Yeah..." And he says, "Well, you did him a big favor by insulting him about his writing." And I say, "Dad, I never insulted him about his writing, I just told him I preferred one draft of a story to another." And my father says, "Well, whatever you said to him, you did him the biggest favor in the world, because after that he gave up wanting to be a writer, and he went to medical school, and he became some kind of research scientist for a series of very prestigious institutions and big biotech companies, and I just learned from his mother that he exercised his stock options and that he's retired, and that he and his wife bought a penthouse at 15 Central Park West and a huge, gorgeous estate in a gated community out in Calabasas, and that they're traveling and skiing and scuba diving and spelunking all over the world." And he says, "I'm really surprised he hasn't called you in all these years and thanked you for insulting his story." And I say, "Well, he's probably too busy spelunking to call, and anyway the cell-phone coverage in caves is pretty shitty." And my dad says, "You're probably right."

And when the Imaginary Intern and I were working on this (and actually we eventually decided not to use it at all because we were becoming increasingly militant about not including any extended anecdotes or vignettes that had any "form"—we were always complaining about the "inanity of form" because, to us, that smacked of "literature" and of "novels," which we were both dead set against, I guess because of the unspeakable things that had happened to us in our lives)...the Imaginary Intern said, "You know what my favorite part of that story is? When you say to your father, 'The cell-phone coverage in caves is pretty shitty,' and he says, 'You're probably right.' I don't know why, or even if this is what you intended, but I thought that was really quite poignant…almost in an artisanal way." And I quoted from Mao's *Talks at the Yan'an Forum on Literature and Art:* "Discard what is backward and develop what is revolutionary," and so that's just what we did, we discarded the whole story. And that's why it's not in the book and that's why you won't be hearing it later tonight.

P.S. When I think back now to Eli's drab, cinder-block dorm room at Tufts, I see a third presence of whom I was unaware when I was actually present there forty years ago. And now the presence persistently haunts this memory…a kind of spectral *roommate* to whom I was oblivious in the empirically verifiable "real world"…a small, round young man with waxy, translucent skin who sat motionless on the edge of his tautly made bed, staring mutely out into space, like a piece of bric-a-brac on a shelf, like a tutelary deity in the bardo world…whose one eye, when I think about it now, was like an aperture into another world…

I finally asked the Imaginary Intern—I think this was about a week or so before he left for good—what exactly he found so moving about that conversation with my father about the cell-phone service in the caves, and he said that sometimes an aging father just doesn't want to argue or have even the mildest disagreement with his son, he just wants everything to feel amiable and copacetic, and if you're being sort of flip and sarcastic, just trying to goad him, and you say something like…and I'm just making this up off the top of my head...something like... "Y'know, Dad, Saint Angela of Foligno drank water contaminated by the putrefying flesh of lepers. Catherine of Siena occasionally sipped pus from cancerous sores. But a Jew? A Jew would *never* drink putrefying leper-water or sip pus from a cancerous sore. *Never happen.* Trust me on that. So if we're just talking about the dramaturgy of self-mortification, you'd have to say that Catholicism is, like, light-years ahead of Judaism." And the aging father, who's sort of half listening at this point, will simply say something very anodyne in response, something very conciliatory, something like "You're probably right." And the Imaginary Intern said, "I just think that's very sweet...again, I just find that to be very poignant...Because it's about someone who just wants to be loving."

This was a side of the Imaginary Intern that you could very easily forget, because he was capable of saying things that were so...what's a good word, uh...so *puerile*. Well, they would seem puerile at first and then later— sometimes much, much later—you'd realize that they weren't puerile at all. He used to always talk about going to a place called Studio Mizuhō, and I just assumed that it was some kind of bar or club or hair salon or something, but I've realized since he left—because I tend to rehash a lot of things he said to me over and over in my head— that Studio Mizuhō is not a place at all, it's a state of heightened awareness and cognition, a state of...of optimized neuroplasticity, memory, focus, computation, analytical ability...a capacity for deep abstraction. So "Let's go to Studio Mizuhō" is really an invitation to sort of jack into this kind of transcendent cognitive nexus where you have, like, total recall and the ability to analyze hundreds of millions of moves per second. But he'd also call this state "Around the Corner Where Fudge Is Made," which is from some silly, scatological rhyme he liked, but it doesn't seem silly or scatological to me at all anymore. It describes to me now a certain specific state of rapture, the state of ecstasy in its original Greek meaning—*ekstasis,* a displacement, a state of being beside one's self or rapt out of one's self. And I use the term at the end of the autobiography—and I'm a little worried that this is something people might not completely get or might misconstrue entirely—when Mussolini comes and picks me up at the mall in the flying balcony, and he asks me where I want to go, I say, "Around the corner where fudge is made." And I don't mean by that up *into* my self. I mean exactly the opposite. I mean that I want to be taken *out* of my self. It describes a way out…as I said, a way out for the mind.

He also used to say—the Imaginary Intern—this funny thing…whenever we'd disagree about something, he'd say, "Let's get our stories straight before the cops get here." Which I just thought was completely adorable. And he'd always point out things to me he knew I loved…We'd be walking down the street, and he'd be like, "Wimpled nuns at ten o'clock"…

It's still a hard thing for me to talk about sometimes, still a painful thing…

Y'know, it will be exactly three years ago this coming Saturday that, sitting on the toilet, I looked down at a pattern of cracks in the tile on my bathroom floor and conjured him up, and almost immediately asked him how he'd feel about collaborating with me on a book about the hedonism of suffering. "How would I feel?" he replied—and I remember this as clearly as if it happened yesterday—he said, "I'm feelin' like a mogul / hittin' jackpots on my mobile," which is a line from a TV ad for online gambling in New Jersey. This was just the way he expressed himself sometimes, in a kind of code or through citations like that.

I mean, he was very enigmatic, which is probably pretty par for the course for a paracosmic entity, but he was also, I think, just very sensitive and very shy. There was a show on Nickelodeon that we watched together once called *Victorious,* and one of the characters was this kid Robbie who had a puppet named Rex, and Robbie did this whole ventriloquist thing...he was a shy kid and the puppet had this brash, sassy personality...and so it enabled Robbie to express himself in ways that he couldn't on his own. And I could see that the show made the Imaginary Intern really uncomfortable. And I couldn't for the life of me figure out why, and I'd even tease him about it and suggest we binge-watch all four seasons...until I realized that it was really bothering him. But I never got an opportunity to sit down and talk to him about it...He left...and...we just never had a chance to...I'm not going to get into all that again, but...Y'know...I could get impatient with him...exasperated some- times...and I never realized back then that his aver- sion to the show, which was ostensibly about the acting and the writing, was...I don't know...veiled or dis- placed...that it really was a sensitivity about playing the role of the ventriloquist's dummy in *our* relation- ship...And my failure to discern that, to acknowledge his insecurities about his own autonomy—something he was far too proud to ever broach explicitly— it pains me still...because I never thought of our relationship in that way, *ever*. The fact is that the Imaginary Intern frequently said things to me, cryptic, puzzling things, that I simply could not have put in his mouth...things I couldn't even fully comprehend at the time he uttered them to me. For instance, once he said: "Autobiography is the Auschwitz of psycholin- guistics." Not in those exact words of course, but that was basically the gist of what he said. And for a long time I tried to work through what that might actu- ally mean. And in the end I think this may be the complete opposite of what I was talking about before. This may actually be something that turned out to be completely specious, that seemed to be abstruse and profound at first, but then turned out to be completely puerile. But I don't care...I still love it.

There are enigmas that we can gnaw on throughout our lives from which we derive sustenance, some kind of spiritual nourishment...I'm thinking of certain kinds of riddles and koans and philosophical conundrums, things like that...But there are also enigmas that, throughout our lives, gnaw on us.

At my bar mitzvah in 1969 (the day before the Jets defeated the Baltimore Colts in the Super Bowl, the game Broadway Joe Namath notoriously predicted the underdog Jets would win), toward the end of the ceremony, the rabbi leaned over and whispered something in my ear. This is something I'd seen him do at each of my friends' bar mitzvahs, and I'd asked them what he said, and it was usually a version of what you might call "words of wisdom"—sometimes a bit platitudinous, but other times, very specific to the boy and his idiosyncrasies and predilections and, in my thirteen-year-old opinion, extremely wise and pertinent, and, again, in my callow opinion (and boys that age do tend to overdramatize and over-romanticize things), perhaps even constituting the essential key to life. And I had a great deal of respect for this rabbi—he was a very personable guy who'd written a highly regarded book about the kabbalah, and I was actually anticipating with avid interest what he was going to whisper to me. I should add here that, for my bar mitzvah, I was wearing this ridiculous multicolor brocade Nehru jacket that my mom had picked out for me...Do you remember that jacket?

MARK'S MOM

You wore that jacket for the party the next day. At the bar mitzvah itself, you wore a regular suit.

MARK

Well, anyway...the rabbi leaned over and he whispered something in my ear, but he was so close to my ear that the words were completely garbled, completely unintelligible, it just sounded like static to me. And I said, "What?" And he did the same thing, put his mouth right up to my ear, too close, and said...said who knows what? It was just more distorted static. And I asked him one more time, "What did you say?" But I could see out of the corner of my eye, some guy—I don't know who it was or what his function was (in my memory's "eye," he's wearing a headset, like the producer on a talk show, but surely that's an interpolation)—and he was making that circular motion in the air with his arm to indicate that we needed to get things moving here, and the rabbi resumed whatever other tasks he needed to resume in order to finish the ceremony.

So what had he said? Was it English, Hebrew, some version of faux-Japanese gibberish (i.e., a kind of placebo wisdom)? Was it some kabbalistic invocation from the Zohar? Was it my secret mantra? Or some banal platitude I could easily live without? I'll never know. Was it—given the fact that life is essentially one long BDSM scene—was it my special safe word that I could use to make it all stop? I did ask him, by the way, a couple of weeks later, but he clearly couldn't remember—I mean the guy did a lot of bar mitzvahs, never mind weddings, funerals, regular sermons, special-event sermons, etc., so I'm not blaming him. But I do feel, to put it simply, that I missed out on my words of wisdom...words of wisdom without which I've struggled and floundered perhaps more than I would have if only the words had been audible to me...and I've maintained this stubborn, completely quixotic... *optimism*, I guess you'd have to call it, that someday the mysterious garbled words will spontaneously emerge in perfect, pristine intelligibility from the sedimentary static in which they've been buried all these years (sort of the way on crime shows they're able to "clean" distorted voices in wiretapped phone conversations), but unfortunately this special message will most likely forever remain in the gnawing-enigma file.

Then, in the eighties, I had a job as a waiter at a place in Jersey City called the Summit House. And one of the first tables I ever waited on was a "deuce," in restaurant lingo, a middle-aged married couple, for whom Friday-night dinner at this particular spot was a custom, a ritual they'd really spruce up for—he always in a carefully pressed polo shirt, seersucker jacket, and dark slacks, she in some sort of floral-print dress, pretty earrings, a pretty tortoiseshell comb in her hair, that sort of thing.

The husband pronounced his *r*'s as *w*'s, a speech defect (sometimes actually a dialect) called *r-labialization*, most famously portrayed, of course, by Elmer Fudd. So, this exceedingly pleasant, exceedingly soft-spoken guy would, each and every Friday evening, invariably order a "Wob Woy, vewy dwy, a wum and Coke for my wife, the pwime wib, vewy ware, and the bwoiled scwod... and would it be possible for my wife to have that with wice instead of Fwench fwies?" he'd politely ask, each and every time.

I never questioned the authenticity of the order. Yes, it seemed improbable that someone who couldn't pronounce the letter *r* would never—just randomly in the course of events—order anything *r*-less, say, a gin and tonic or a scotch or a steak or a veal chop or spaghetti and meatballs or a chicken pot pie. But I just figured he knew what he liked, knew what his wife liked, and that was that. He seemed like a perfectly decent sort of guy. And I had absolutely no reason to doubt his sincerity. And there'd almost always be dessert—the inevitable "bwead pudding and wed velvet cake"—and at least two "bwandies." All of which added up to a hefty check for two people, with a potentially substantial tip. So you want to be as accommodating as possible.

One Friday night—this must have been after waiting on them for two or three weeks in a row—the husband asked me some variation on the question, Assuming you don't want to be a professional waiter all your life, what do you really want to do? And I said that I wanted to

be a writer someday. And he said that he and his wife
love to "wead." And I asked, "Who are your favorite
writers?" He thought for a moment and he said, "I love
Joseph Conwad, Waymond Chandler...and especially
Gwaham Gweene." Now at this point, I remember, I did
look around, feeling momentarily that I might be being
punked in some way, in some sort of *Candid Camera* stunt
or something, that someone had put him up to this. But
again, I really had no reason to think—in fact it seemed
a little crazy for me to think—that this seemingly guile-
less person was in on some sort of elaborate prank that
was taking weeks to develop...and who'd want to do
this to me anyway? I barely knew any of the other wait-
ers or staff at this place. But still, no *r*-less writers? No
Melville, no Poe, no Hemingway...just "Conwad" and
"Gweene"? I mean, c'mon. What are the odds here?

I was just about to head back to the kitchen to pick
up one of my other tables' orders, when the guy said,
"I also love music." I took a deep breath. "Oh," I said.
"What kinds of music?" And again he thought for a mo-
ment or two, and then he said, "I love the Wamones,
Woxy Music...and especially"—and this he said in a
much louder, more declarative voice—"especially Guns
N' Woses."

And at this moment, I was positive that I heard people sniggering, that there were little contingents of my
cohorts huddled in corners of the dining room barely
able to control their laughter. And I felt this radiant heat
rising from the back of my neck and I felt as if my face

must have been bright, bright red with humiliation. And although I never actually saw anyone laughing at me, I knew that they were. *Who* they were and *why* they did that to me, I'll never know. And, yes, it's *possible* that a middle-aged man from Jersey City with r-labialization could like "Wob Woys," "pwime wib," "Gwaham Gweene," and "Guns N' Woses," but it's such a remote possibility as to be pretty much inconceivable. Someone . . . or some people . . . were behind all this, and their identities will also remain forever in the gnawing-enigma file.

And I also think that this particular event . . . I guess because I felt so abjectly alone, so on display at that moment, in that dining room full of people (in *that* particular "food court") . . . that this event not only instilled in me a wariness and a hypervigilance and suspiciousness, and maybe even paranoia, that have never abated, but also a weird, masochistic love of precisely this sort of public humiliation. And I'm not saying that's necessarily a *good* thing or a *bad* thing, I'm just saying that that's probably why we're all here tonight, and, again, I'm extremely grateful for the opportunity.

The earliest known jokes had no punch lines. They simply consisted of a setup. For example: "A man and a woman exit a garden in shame." In other words, there were no writers. Today, on the other hand, *everyone* is a writer. I heard a guy say the other day, "My nuts don't fit into H&M jeans." That's funny, but that doesn't make him a writer. That would be like calling yourself a gang-ster because you kill the germs that cause bad breath. To call yourself a writer (and this has absolutely nothing to do with whether you actually write anything or not), you have to imprison yourself in your adolescent bed-room for several years, forcing Kundalini energy up your spinal column until your mind is launched from your body.

Those sounds we hear at regular intervals in our dreams (that some have likened to the sounds of the Ōtsuzumi drum in Noh) are actually the black-box pings of our own errant minds.

Dreams are subject to all the wanton dissimulations of the mischievous psyche, which produce distinct levels of latent and manifest content. I have a recurring dream about my childhood hero, Mickey Mantle. I'm in Yan-kee Stadium, sitting in a box seat at dugout level right near home plate, and Mantle comes up at bat, and he launches the first pitch deep into the center-field bleachers, and he turns, and, in slow motion and in that slowed-down distorted voice, he beckons to me to come join him in his home-run trot around the bases. So I immediately start trying to clamber out of the box, and it's one of those frustrating sequences in a dream where, for some inexplicable reason, you can't seem to get your body to do the simple thing you're trying to get it to do, and it takes what seems like innumerable attempts and an impossibly protracted period of time to pull myself over that railing, and then when I do finally succeed in climbing out onto the field, my wallet must fall out of the back pocket of my pants, because I feel for it later in the dream and it's not there. So, I'm maybe ten feet behind Mantle and I'm trotting behind him to first base, and he looks back at me, and he seems really crazy, he has this floridly psychotic look on his face, and then he doesn't make the turn to second, he just keeps going, he just continues along the right-field foul line, and soon we're out of the stadium entirely, and we're running and we're running, and he's getting further and further ahead of me, until I can't see him anymore, but I'm still following that same vector, and now I'm going through all these shifting landscapes—city, country, mountains, jungle, desert. And I realize a funny thing—every couple of minutes, I'm passing the exact same things: a bus stop, a strip mall, a factory, a farm stand, the ruins of the same Mayan temple, the same couple of Bedouins at an oasis, the same sad clowns, the same group of tantric sadhus with their three-pronged trident staffs, marigolds, and red hibiscus flowers, the same gas-station minimart with its baleful Indian chief...then the whole sequence all over again. It's like the looping, wraparound backgrounds they used to use in early animation and racing video games. And I realize—*as* I'm dreaming—that the production values of the dream totally suck, that obviously I can only afford a handful of shitty locations and have to keep using them over and over and over again. So not only is my chagrin about the repeating locations the most phantasmagorical part of the dream—because realistically in a dream one can obviously "afford" any location—it is also the part of the dream most laden with meaning for me, depicting, as it does, the shame I feel about my financial fecklessness and perennial insolvency.

The Imaginary Intern was vehemently opposed to the inclusion of dreams in the autobiography. He was completely, intransigently hard-line about this. We were always talking about the need to renounce counterrevolutionary forms, and the Imaginary Intern maintained, and he was unswerving about this to the very day he disappeared, withdrew, quit, whatever you want to call it...he maintained—he was *adamant* about this—that expository dreams were counterrevolutionary, that they comprise the same form as anecdotes and vignettes, which we both despised as "literary" and which we were both violently opposed to including in the autobiography. We had discovered during the, uh...during the, the *gestation* of the autobiography, that it was the segues and the interstices, the oblique and incidental details, all the throwaway, offhand remarks and obiter dicta that invariably ended up being the most meaningful, the most weirdly hyper-cathected stuff—just our favorite stuff—in the whole book. We pledged to abide by the injunction "Tell, don't show," and its corollary "Diagnose, don't tell." "We are not writers," he'd say. "We are clinicians." Dreams are simply a means of smuggling literary modes and motifs into the autobiography. Dreams (i.e., narrative dreams) "wave the red banner to oppose the red banner," meaning that they have a specious allure, they seem "all trippy and schizzed out," but they utilize counterrevolutionary expository elements. Literary content, he'd say, is "a nodular accumulation of yellowish, cheesy sebaceous material that can harden into large plaques."

The Imaginary Intern claimed to only have nonexpository dreams (or "dremes," as he called them). He said—and again, his diction tended to be very juvenile and somewhat ghetto, so I'm paraphrasing here—he said that his dreams were a sort of kinesthesia of mathematical torsions and arabesques and fractals, and could never be represented in language, that they eluded and exceeded rational transmission, that they were pure quivering, contingent thought in its barest provisionality...an evanescing froth that represented the abolition of meaning in favor of form.

The whole question of whether or how a dreamt-up entity dreams is a fascinating one that I actually pursued with him at great length...and, uh...I was thinking this is something you guys might want to possibly explore further with me in the Q and A later...

(The "guys" remain emphatically uninterested.)

MARK

There was definitely, I have to admit, an anti-Semitic strain to some of the Imaginary Intern's ideas about this, to some of his beliefs. He'd occasionally use the word *Jewification*. He'd talk about the Jewification of dreams through the importing, the transplantation of literary motifs, etc. This would usually happen when we were both high on oxycodone... although I know that's no excuse.

(MARK glances guiltily at his MOM, then back at the fast-food workers.)

MARK

Did either of you guys happen see that movie *Lake Little Lake* that was on TV...I think it was Saturday...on Lifetime...pretty sure it was Lifetime...this past Saturday night... *Lake Little Lake?* Did you guys see that?... No?...

I've never seen a movie that makes being chemically castrated seem so appealing.

Neither of you guys saw that...last Saturday...no?

(MARK sighs, flagging somewhat, seeming, for the first time, a little discouraged.)

MARK

I'm trying, Mom...I really am.

(MARK'S MOM mouths the words I know you are.*)*

MARK

Sometimes when we were drinking, the Imaginary Intern would mumble ominous things to me...his back turned...a silhouette...But he was crying this one time.

"What's the matter?" I asked him.

"I'm worried about you," he said. "You have a powerful death drive—it's a nostalgia for a lost harmony, a desire to return to a pre-Oedipal fusion with your mother's breast. Have you been having any fantasies of castration and self-destruction lately...fantasies that you're finding it harder and harder not to act upon?"

"Why? Would that be bad?"

"It's completely normal. Relax."

"A child's been abandoned on a merry-go-round in the middle of the night in a desolate, crepuscular de Chirico–like landscape. The seats on the merry-go-round are not the usual horses, they're hagfish, pygmy marmosets, Madagascar sucker-footed bats, that sort of thing. There are no other human beings anywhere, with the exception of a woman (the child's mother, we'll soon learn) who recedes in the distance, arm in arm with a disreputable-looking guy in a white wifebeater and greasy blue overalls, a cigarette lodged above one ear. Suddenly two glowing dots...these two tiny punctiform gleams appear in the distant black sky—the rabid eyes of some sort of winged reptile which grow larger and larger as the creature gets closer and closer, and the calliope music grows louder and more dissonant and more demented. I can see now, of course, that this terrified child is me, because he's tiny, he has wispy blond bangs, and he's dressed in this ridiculous multicolor brocade Nehru jacket. Suddenly the creature is upon the child, he's torn him open with one savage slash of his glinting talon, and he's yanking loops of intestine from the child's abdomen as he screams in agony for his mother, who, as we hear the Velvet Underground crooning 'She's a femme fatale' in the background, disappears into the horizon with her louche drifter boyfriend."

"Dude, I *love* that song."

He extended a fist that I bumped with mine.

"How does it feel while you're being eviscerated by this, this creature?" he asked.

"It's like I'm being unspooled...it sort of conjures up the unraveling of my father's and mother's DNA in the zygote at the end of the *Gone with the Mind* video game."

We cracked open two more cold Spaten lagers.

"Does it hurt—the disemboweling?"

"It's a strange sensation...not agonizing at all actually, not even painful really...but not pleasurable...it's a very, very peculiar feeling...but the whole regime of obligation seems to disintegrate, as if adhesions and knots of scar tissue are coming loose...I feel as if I'm diffusing into the flux, diffusing in and through language, in and through verbs, if that makes any sense...And I feel as if this is the crossroads to which all other paths in my life have been leading. Do you know what I mean?"

"I do, absolutely. First of all, I think the horizon represents the spurious line separating hysteria and politics. And I think being torn apart by a prehistoric winged reptile symbolizes for you an ecstatic capitulation to imperious events beyond your control—in other words, a way out... a way out for your mind. And it's not hard to see the correlation between disembowelment and the a posteriori disgorging of one's contents that *is* autobiography... How does it feel seeing your mother disappear with that lowlife scumbag who's got his hand down her pants?"

(MARK clasps his hands to his heart and gives his MOM the most fervent look of esteem and affection one could possibly imagine.)

MARK

I think that mother is the most virtuous woman in the world. I venerate that mother. I salute her Maoist *nostalgie de la boue.*

Tonight I salute that mother's magnificent refusal to be buried alive... and her implacable resolve to transform that resistance into discourse.

(MARK'S MOM bows her head in appreciation.)

MARK

Okay, last couple of things before I get started...

In 1966, my grandmother Harriet took me and my cousin Adam to the Stanley Theater in Jersey City to see *One Million Years B.C.* starring Raquel Welch, who spoke only three lines of dialogue, but wore a mammoth-fur bikini for the entire movie. And at some juncture during the film, when Welch attempts to fend off a pterodactyl with a big stick, my grandmother started laughing. And I really don't know what she found so funny, but she laughed so hard, so helplessly at this, that she peed in her pants. Now, although this is a fairly typical example of what they call *enuresis risoria*, or giggle enuresis, it made a big impression on me, it really did inscribe itself in the soft cement of my juvenile mind. And I...I mention this only because, in looking over my notes in the car on the way over here tonight, I realized that several of the excerpts I'm going to read—most of them, actually— revolve around this whole nexus between paleo- ornithology and urinary incontinence, and I just thought it might be helpful for you guys if you knew the origin of all that, and also how it sort of prefigures not only my own interim catheterization following the robotic prostatectomy, but the impending diluvial catas- trophe alluded to by my mom in her introduction.

When I was a child, the only place where my mother could actually "abandon" me without fearing for my sanity—without fearing that, in my wild grief, I might

rip out my own entrails and stuff them into my mouth—
was Lord & Taylor. I would just sit there among the
mannequins, as patient and as perfectly tranquil as they
were, and wait for her to shop, forging in my mind
the link between death and theater. Imagine the lucid
stillness of that tableau...that fey boy with his wispy
bangs, finally in his milieu, finally among his peers—
those mute inanimate figures, cataleptically casual in
their permanent-press sportswear, their minds so far
away. And I'd think about what songs I wanted played
at my funeral—of course, the Civil War songs that I
so adored listening to at that age, that I listened to so
obsessively..."John Brown's Body," "All Quiet Along
the Potomac," "Hard Times Come Again No More."
And when, in high school, like the lobotomized protagonist of some teen drama, I fell under the sway of
a periodontist's daughter named Elizabeth Ross, who'd
spent several summers at the Interlochen Arts Camp
in Michigan, I became partial to the larghetto second
movement of Mozart's Piano Concerto no. 27 in B-flat
Major, Mozart's last piano concerto (this was during a
period in my life when I was very much trying to de-
vise a new identity for myself, and insisted on people
calling me "Dick Al Dente" [an alias betokening the am-
bivalence about the sexual awakening of someone who
already yearned nostalgically for the slumber of inno-
cence]). The music I now want played at my funeral
is Robyn's song "Call Your Girlfriend." I know, right?!
(Dream scenario—Robyn herself comes and performs

the song live at some decrepit funeral home under a highway overpass in Jersey City. Otherwise, I've got it on my iPhone.) I know to some of you this probably seems like a silly, arbitrary, kind of gay choice...I mean, the song isn't elegiac or wistful, it's not a rumination on mortality and finitude, it's not valedictory in any sense, there's no bittersweet retrospection or tallying of regrets, it isn't a celebration of life or the oceanic feeling of cosmic interconnectivity or anything even remotely like that. What "Call Your Girlfriend" is—in case you're some sort of dense fuck who doesn't know anything about music—is a super-catchy electropop synth ballad about a love triangle, addressed by a woman to a guy she's seeing, urging him to call his current girlfriend and have "the talk" about how he's met somebody new, and about how different it is when they kiss, and let her down easy and break up.

(He winks at the PANDA EXPRESS WORKER and the SBARRO WORKER, indicating that he considers them members of the cognoscenti and not dense fucks.)

MARK

And even if it ends up just being you two guys and my mom at the funeral, I can *so* imagine that song playing and I'm lying there in my coffin, my hair slicked back, in my Alex Rodriguez Yankee jersey and my plaid pajama bottoms, the outfit I wore when we (the Imaginary Intern and I) composed *Gone with the Mind,* which was *our* last piano concerto, the outfit which was my version of *prozodezhda,* the "production clothing" worn by the great Russian constructivist Aleksandr Rodchenko—the original A-Rod.

Y'know, I was sitting next to this guy at a bar the other night, and he's, uh...he's telling me...a stranger, a guy I never met before...he's telling me this story about how his wife must have spent, like, four hours in the store, in some CVS or Walmart, finding a birthday card for him that evinced absolutely no feeling whatsoever and had absolutely no relevance to him. And they make these cards specifically so they seem to apply to everyone, so they're germane and emotionally resonant to absolutely anyone! They're like horoscopes in that way, they're *always* right. But somehow, this woman, his wife, had taken the time and scrupulously searched out a birthday card for a husband that was completely cold, completely emotionally detached and dissociated, without *any* correlation to *anything* in his life. And I think he was actually proud of her...that this was his way of boasting about how persevering and conscientious she was, that she'd expend that kind of effort finding a birthday card, probably the one birthday card in that entire store, so completely purged of any true feeling or relevance, but still acknowledging the occasion. And I realized that he was maligning his wife (as husbands frequently do in bars and barbershops) as a way of flattering her, as a way of exalting her and thus elevating himself, which is pretty fucked up, but that's the problem with hanging out in bars that are overpopulated with men, you have to listen to a lot of fucked-up shit like this. But it did make me think about whether, if one could completely drain a birthday card of emotion and still have a birthday card and completely purge a funeral song of lament and wistfulness and still have a funeral song...whether one could eradicate all the quaint handicraft synonymous with an autobiography (the anecdotes, the vignettes, the euphonious composition of literary motifs) and—as the Imaginary Intern and I were fanatically committed to doing—still have an autobiography. (Of course, only you guys can be the true judges of whether or not we've succeeded, once you've had a chance to hear the excerpts.)

It's very interesting all the transference and countertransference that can go on between two strangers drinking together at bar, and I found myself telling the guy about how, when I was a little boy, my grandfather Raymond (my mom's dad) gave me a card—a store-bought, Hallmark card *he* presumably took the time to search out at a drugstore somewhere or other—congratulating me for receiving a Cub Scout merit badge, the one I was awarded for extinguishing my den mother's hair which she'd set on fire lighting her cigarette off the stove-top burner, that whole business, which I think particularly pleased my grandfather because it undergirded his contention that cigarettes were a "filthy habit," something he repeated with the distaste of a convert, having smoked two packs of unfiltered Chesterfields a day for the entirety of his adult life until making a bet with a colleague who said he couldn't quit, and never smoking another cigarette from that moment on ever again.

Intellectual histories tend to underestimate the importance of blows to the head. Occasionally we hear about a rare case of acquired savant syndrome in which prodigious mental skills emerge after a brain injury, typically an injury to the left anterior temporal lobe, where there's a subsequent recruitment and rewiring of still-intact cortical tissue resulting in a release of dormant potential. And didn't we all as schoolchildren impishly suspect that Newton's legendary flash of intuition as he sat under a tree in his mother's garden in 1666, his great epiphany about gravitation, was the result of a traumatic brain injury caused by the falling apple that hit him in the head? But I really think—I *know*, actually, from personal experience—that the phenomenon is much more prevalent than has been reported, and I think the government is suppressing this out of fear that young writers, our most gifted, most impish young writers (by whom I mean those who write the most beautiful code) would keep mallets in their little cubbyholes and bludgeon themselves when feeling blocked or fallow. And then there are the older ones, like me, in their improvised ateliers—their bathrooms and their cars—and here it's less a bludgeoning than a metronomic tap-tap-

tap ... a metronomic tap-tap-tap, submerged in the concentric clamor of the day. That's probably the best way I can express how I feel like nothing and everything at the same time ... a metronomic tap-tap-tap, submerged in the concentric clamor of the day.

In the summer of 1967, in the front yard of our shore house at 73 Neptune Avenue in Deal, New Jersey, my grandfather Raymond hit me in the head, flush in the forehead, with a baseball. He was a strong, barrel-chested, bandy-legged guy, and I remember him winding up ... he had this crazy, elaborate, sort of contorted Luis Tiant–style windup ... and I can still picture this old three-fingered, linseed-stained mitt he had ... he wound up, delivered his high cheese, and I didn't even have the chance to reflexively raise my glove to protect myself. They didn't have radar speed guns in those days, but I'm estimating he hit me in the head with a sixty-five-mile-an-hour fastball.

And it knocked me out cold. And there I was, lying unconscious on the ground ... like some poor street kid hit by a rubber bullet in a restive favela, a poor, woozy, little blond, daydreamy cabbage-patch sphinx, mouth agape, drooling—had I wet my pants just a bit?—and in the violent recoil of my head, my mind's eyeball ricocheted forward, a projectile hurtling into the future. And the women present—my mother, my aunt, my grandmother—were screaming and they'd all instinctively lurched toward my limp, crumpled body, and my grandfather warned them, in his resounding voice,

against coming any closer, "He's fine. Don't be idiots."
But my mother just flung him aside, she just flung him
aside, like he was nothing. And when I came to—and
I can remember this so vividly, the air a heavy haze of
mint and honeysuckle, blurred by the heat and the vi-
brations of bees and dragonflies—I was cradled in her
arms, this time very much as sons are cradled by their
Marys in Pietà sculptures, though, today, in retrospect, it
reminds me so much more of that wonderfully Oedipal
scene in *White Heat* when the deranged, psychopathic
gangster Cody Jarrett (played by James Cagney) has one
of his seizures and keels over onto the floor in front of his
crew, and his mother, Ma Jarrett (Margaret Wycherly),
manages to steer him into the bedroom of this cabin
they're holed up in, and he says to her, "It's like having
a red-hot buzz saw inside my head," and she massages
the back of his neck until he's feeling better and ready
to go back out into the living room, but she says, "No,
not yet, son. Don't let 'em see you like this. Might give
some of 'em ideas," and Cody sits on her lap and he
says, "You're always thinkin' about your Cody, aren't
ya?" and his mom gets up and pours him a glass of
whiskey, and says, "Top of the world, son," and Cody
says, "Don't know what I'd do without ya, Ma," and he
knocks back the whiskey, and his mom says, "Now go
on out there, and show 'em you're all right." I know
that scene by heart. That's one of my favorite scenes of
all time (that and the closet scene with Hamlet and his
mother, Gertrude). And I think that even in my life now,

even tonight here at the food court, I'm still trying to just go out there and show 'em that I'm all right.

In that moment, when I regained consciousness on the lawn of that house in my mother's arms, I immediately realized that I was a different person. It was a moment of germination, a crossroads. I do very much believe that being hit in the head with that baseball marked the beginning for me of the *vita contemplativa,* of my *amor dei intellectualis,* that very instant I crossed the threshold into Studio Mizuhō. And though I was only eleven at the time (and obviously didn't have the vocabulary then to adequately articulate these kinds of things), those matters which would preoccupy me for the rest of my life crystallized in my mind in that instant, on impact: To express that which only the futility of language can express, and that only the specific futility of this specific language can express. And to contest in a particularly expert manner the domain of the expert; to contest in a particularly exceptional and artistic manner, the domain of the exceptional artist.

There's a didactic purpose behind almost everything a parent or a grandparent does. If your father runs you over with his own car, it's probably to teach you not to nap in the driveway. If he's been drinking and he stabs you with a fork, it's probably to teach you not to get too close to drunk people while they're eating. Of course, you don't realize this when you're a child, you just assume you're being tormented. When I was that age, I identified very strongly with persecuted minorities, among which, in my accursed singularity, I considered myself the most ruthlessly persecuted. And it probably seemed to me that my grandfather was just being a cretin who got off on treating me like one of those milk bottles you knock down for prizes at a carnival. But I'm sure he was trying to teach me to pay attention when you're playing catch with someone instead of staring up at zeppelins, which I had a tendency to do. But my mom, reluctant to expose me to repeated blows to the head, gently discouraged me from playing catch with my grandfather ever again. "You don't want to get chronic traumatic encephalopathy, do you?" she asked. "Gosh, Mom... I guess not." As I stand here before you tonight, I can remember exactly what she was wearing at that very moment—a blue-and-yellow-striped tunic top, gray clam-digger pants, and flats—compelling evidence, I believe, that I do *not* suffer from chronic traumatic encephalopathy. And allow me to offer one final "fuck everyone who said I was too brain-traumatized to succeed in life" (even though they were probably right).

You wouldn't know from my grandfather's Anglophilic affectations—the rolling of his *r*'s (most ostentatiously when providing telephone operators with a number he wanted to reach, always including the exchange name, in this booming, stentorian voice, so everyone within several blocks could hear, "I'd like you to connect me to Henderson thrrree, five-thrrree-seven-thrrree"), the incessant citations of Shaw and Wilde, and the fetishistic touting of various British products

(Wilkinson razor blades, Burberry raincoats, Lock & Company homburgs, Boodles gin, Fortnum's marmalade, etc.)—that this was a man who'd been born in Estonia and brought to Jersey City at the age of one. Although there was one American-made product for which he had a zealous lifelong predilection—those big shiny Cadillacs with the enormous tail fins, the de Villes and the Eldorados. He loved tooling around Jersey City and Deal in a gleaming new Caddie. And he'd say to me, "Markie, my boy, shall we take the Cadillac for a bath?" And I'd jump up and down like a little puppy, because I loved going through car washes, and I still do. I always come out of a car wash in a better mood than I went in with. (And I have to add here, without getting maudlin all over again, that it was while going through a car wash that the Imaginary Intern and I came up with the idea of including my Minnesota Multiphasic Personality Inventory report in the autobiography.) My grandfather had three notorious expressions he used habitually: "If your grandmother had balls, she'd be your grandfather," "Crept into the crypt, crapped, and crept out again," and "Let's not and say we did." The first one, "If your grandmother had balls, she'd be your grandfather," was used to preempt any kind of thinking he considered overly speculative. I'm not exactly sure what "Crept into the crypt, crapped, and crept out again" was ever apropos of, but, for me, it spoke of the scatological and the eschatological, and it's really stuck with me, and if I'm ever asked for advice by young wannabe writers (which, by the way, I will *never* be), I'd tell them, *If you find yourself at an impasse, when you're stumped, and that, y'know ... that blank white page, that empty screen is just sort of glaring back at you, go with scatology and eschatology. You just really can't go wrong with scatology and eschatology.* My favorite expression of his, though, the one I found to be most enduringly evocative was "Let's not and say we did," and I remember hoping that someday soon he'd ask me if I wanted to do something (like taking the Cadillac for a bath) and I'd have the gumption to respond "Let's not and say we did," using his own pithy demurrer against him (as in the days of nineteenth-century surgery, when un-anesthetized patients, half crazed with unimaginable pain, would leap off the operating table and attack the surgeons with their own instruments), but I never had the heart to do it back then. I was an extremely sensitive little boy. I mean, I was so sensitive that even books— *especially* books—could cause me terrific apprehension. I would stare up at the books in my grandparents' living room at 1904 Hudson Boulevard (now Kennedy Boulevard), and almost tremble ... shelf after shelf, all the way up to the ceiling, of these august volumes, this wall of books that seemed to lean, to teeter menacingly towards me, as I stood there gazing up, as if at the edifice of a temple, as if it might just crush me with the sheer power of the cultural endorsement represented by these tomes, crush me in the aggregate gravitas of all its exalted, erudite authors, who wielded an intellectual prowess that I could never really even comprehend, never mind possess myself. For some reason, only the encyclopedia seemed congenial to me, within my grasp, and for some reason—and who can really understand the twisted psyches of little children—my favorite thing in the entire multivolume set of encyclopedias, the thing to which I'd return over and over again, with a compulsive regularity, to which I was almost fatally impelled to gaze upon on every visit, was a sepia-toned photograph of an African man with elephantiasis of the testicles who had to walk around with his hideously enormous balls in a wheelbarrow. And sometimes I'd wander over to the credenza where Ray would mix his daily martini, and the long glass rod stirrer he used would seem to me, to this sickly child prone to ear infections, like some sort of Grand Guignol rectal thermometer, another talismanic object that filled me with both dread and desire.

When I slept over at my grandparents' house, which was only a few blocks away from ours on Westminster Lane, I'd wake up extra early so I could observe his toilette. I was fascinated, I was enraptured by this transformation. I'd watch, with a kind of awed wonder, his production of himself each morning, by the complete sociobiological metamorphosis from the rumpled, musty-smelling little man I'd glimpse emerging from my grandparents' bedroom into that great, gleaming, redoubtable, fragrant narcissist. He listened to WINS news on a little transistor radio in a calfskin case as he shaved every morning, splashed on his Vétiver, ate his breakfast, and, galvanized by his coffee and his boiled egg into that great man of action, that great public man, emerged later in Journal Square, where common men paid him obeisance and addressed him as Counselor or Consigliere and he greeted them back with his noblesse oblige, rolling his *r*'s. He was to me then a splendid, formidable, charismatic sight to behold, a man who'd been known all over Jersey City as someone with the temerity to stand up to the powerful political machine of Frank "I Am the Law" Hague (I was born in Margaret Hague Hospital, the maternity hospital named after his mother), though, there was for me, even at that age, ironically, something of the boss, something of Il Duce about Ray himself. He was most floridly, most grandly and exultantly himself in the piazza. In Journal Square. In public. He seemed to chafe at the constraints of domesticity. We'd drive in his shiny Cadillac past those little canals in Kearny or Secaucus, those iridescent slurries of mercury and PCBs, the classical station WQXR blaring from the radio at head-splitting volume... It's amazing, isn't it, how perfectly this big-balled Duce from Estonia steering his gleaming Eldorado with its deafening Puccini past psychedelic streams of toxic sludge presages Mussolini piloting his flying balcony through the polychromatic concourses of this mall at the very end of *Gone with the Mind*? It's amazing how so much of this was already there, intact, back then... how so much of it was already written.

When he got older, he developed a tendency to make these odd, completely gratuitous telephone calls, these peremptory rebukes that would just come out of nowhere. The phone would ring, you'd answer, and, without so much as a hello, he'd snarl, "Why aren't you watching Golda Meir on *Face the Nation,* you dumb bastard?!" And he'd hang up. Or "If you're not watching Itzhak Perlman on *Good Morning America,* you're a goddamn moron!" Click. It almost seemed to me that, though he was still alive, Ray was already speaking from beyond, that this was some kind of transdimensional ventriloquism, that he'd thrown his voice into the land of the dead and it had ricocheted back somehow into the mouth of my superego, as my own voice of judgment and accusation. To me there was an undeniable sort of verve or élan to the calls, these batty pranks that were so perfectly punctuated by that concussive hang-up. But there were people in my family—*most* of the people in my family, I guess—who found these calls particularly unamusing, who thought they were just jarring and mean. But I liked them. I *needed* them, actually. I really think they helped me get through a couple of rough years…Just imagine standing on a subway platform in the morning, terribly hungover, and some demented person stabs you in the buttocks with an EpiPen, and you're kind of like, "Thanks." That's what it was like for me getting these calls. At the very least, one began to suspect that his mind was chafing at the constraints of his body. But as much as his health deteriorated, he never completely abandoned the piazza, refusing to relinquish his status as a public being, stubbornly performing that role even in its abjection, incorporating all his mortifying indignities, his hydrocele, his colostomy bag, the blend of feces and Vétiver left in his wake, these conspicuous signs of morbidity, without any shame, in fact with a perverse kind of pride and vanity. And though we all cringed and commiserated with each other about how unpleasant and sad it had all become, I find this to be, the more I age and atrophy and putrefy myself, especially in this culture that so valorizes the alleged virtues of youth and health…I find this—Ray's sad and stubborn "encore"—the more and more that I think about it, to be something splendid, something spectacular.

The last time I saw him, he was dying, in a room at Christ Hospital in Jersey City…He was lying there, shrunken, wheezing, his eyes wide and bulging with fear and surprise, and I couldn't help but think of something I'd stumbled upon one night by the lake at a summer camp in the Adirondacks—a frog in the gaping jaws of a snake, its eyes wide and bulging, as it was inexorably drawn into the abyss by the snake's peristalsis. And my mom said to my grandfather…and I don't even know why I was privy to this, an interloper to such intimacy…she said to him, "Dad, we've had such wonderful times together…You can let go now…You don't have to fight so hard." And I thought it was the most magnificent, the bravest thing I'd ever seen her do. And you know what a magnificent, brave person I think she is. But I also thought, why do we have to wait until we're literally dying, until we're already in the jaws of the serpent, for some loving, benevolent person to say to us, "You can stop fighting so hard. It's okay. Let go"? And this "letting go" is one of the things we (the Imaginary Intern and I) mean by *Gone with the Mind*.

By this time—and it almost seemed as if years had passed since he told me the story about his wife picking out that birthday card for him—the guy at the bar and I had had so much to drink that we were arm in arm, singing...alternating between a child's piping soprano and a grandfather's imposing baritone—

Do you want to live off the grid...like a yid, in Madrid?
Let's not...Let's not and say we did.
Would you like to eat squid, in a pyramid...with Billy the Kid?
Let's not...Let's not and say we did.

When I was a little boy, I was so sensitive that the sound of beautiful music—like "This Diamond Ring" by Gary Lewis and the Playboys or "I'm Telling You Now" by Freddie and the Dreamers or "Game of Love" by Wayne Fontana and the Mindbenders—would make me physically ill. During one of the summers that I went to that camp up in the Adirondacks—I must have been about ten—we took a little day trip to Lake George. I'll never forget being in a gift shop up there, one of those touristy places that sells all sorts of goofy trinkets and T-shirts and stuff...and that song "Red Rubber Ball" by the Cyrkle came on the radio...and when it got to that part "The roller-coaster ride we took is nearly at an end / I bought my ticket with my tears, that's all I'm gonna spend," I just lost it...I'd been missing my parents terribly, the kids in my bunk had been picking on me quite a bit, and they'd nicknamed me Tweezers which, to this day, I don't understand...and the "we" in that line about the roller-coaster ride, I, of course, took to mean me and my mom...in other words, that the beautiful, sanctified time with my mom was over, and I also interpreted that to betoken the mortality of my existence as a child, and I just couldn't bear that thought...I still feel as if almost everything I do is a kind of desperate, irredentist maneuver to recover that lost territory from oblivion, to recuperate that Eden, that once-upon-a-time...and I sort of slumped to the floor of the gift shop in tears, and I remember vividly the cloying, almost suffocating aroma of taffy and candy-coated nuts, and my weird, freckle-faced, perverted counselor from Alabama coming over to console me.

From the very first day of summer camp...from the very minute I stepped off that bus...this guy began trying to cultivate a "special" relationship with me... primarily by constantly taking me aside and, very confidentially, feeding me some piece of racist and prurient misinformation including the assertion that black people had larger sex organs than white people. I wasn't even entirely sure what a sexual organ actually was at the time. He said he had a photograph which proved it, would I like to see it? And I said, Okay, sure. And this is going to be hard for you to believe, but it's true, I fucking swear on the life of my mother...He showed me the photograph of the African man with the elephantiasis of the testicles, and he told me *all* black men had balls this size. And for a number of years after that, I'd look, y'know, I'd try to check, which got me into a lot of trouble...staring at black men's crotches and wondering how they managed to somehow fit their colossal, wheelbarrow-worthy balls into their pants, thinking perhaps it was somehow akin to the way a Rastafarian might fit his enormous trove of dreadlocks into his crocheted cap...And as soon as I got home from camp that particular summer, I immediately went over to my grandparents' house at 1904 Hudson Boulevard and immediately rushed over to the set of encyclopedias on the bookshelf, took down the E volume, flipping the pages in an agitated panic to the entry for elephantiasis, because I'd completely convinced myself that this creepy counselor (whose name I've repressed) had somehow snuck into my grandparents' house, clipped out the photo of the guy with his balls in the wheelbarrow, and snuck out again...a real-life version of someone creeping into a crypt, crapping, and creeping out again. But, of course, the photo was still there...the page, at least, unmolested.

*   *   *

When the Imaginary Intern said, "I'm worried about you," I felt like saying to him, *I'm worried about* you. There were times, as I said, when he'd mumble ominous things to me and just...just sulk, y'know? He was kind of like a precocious child, but a child nonetheless. Well...let me put it this way: he was like a precocious child who had turned into a morbid adolescent...well, a reclusive adolescent with morbid compulsions (it's almost impossible obviously to describe the Imaginary Intern without describing myself).

One time he got this eerie look on his face, as if he were holding a flashlight under his chin, and he said in this heavy Japanese accent, "I am the ghost of your dead sister." And then he switched to this sort of posh Indian accent. "You realize, don't you, that the only part of your life that the autobiography actually represents is the time that elapsed as you wrote it...the time with me...your autobiography is actually a biography of me."

"Why do you think I'm obsessed with this idea of giving the world an alphabet-soup enema?" (This was our code language for wanting to be a writer.)

After a very long, Viennese pause, he said, "Why do *you* think you are?"

And I said, "I don't know...Prolonged exposure to radiation from violent events in deep space?"

When he'd say things to me like "I'm the ghost of your dead sister," I didn't take it all that seriously. I think he was just trying to seem more badass than he really was. I mean, it's more impressive, more exciting, "cooler" I suppose, to say "I'm the ghost of your dead sister" than "I'm an imaginary entity conjured up from cracks in bathroom tile." You know what I mean? I get that. It did occur to me sometimes that he was less a co-producer, less a collaborator on the autobiography and more a product or a by-product of the autobiography, almost like (and I'd never say this to him)... almost like some sort of teratoma which flourishes in the favorable nutrient medium of childhood retrospection. Nonetheless, I hated seeing him sulk, hated feeling that he was dissatisfied in any way...

I said to him once, "You're an Imaginary Intern, you know... you're not an Imaginary Indentured Slave. You're free to leave whenever you like. I just want you to be happy."

He let out a sigh and gazed down at the ground for a moment. "I am happy," he murmured.

"I want you to know something," I said. "I love you. And I'm never going to lie about you or be ashamed of you or anything like that, okay?"

As I've said before, the Imaginary Intern talked like a kid, so you had to wade through—just to give you a good example—all his diffident phumphering, all the "he was like, *Blah-blah,* and she was all like, *Blah-blah-blah,*" all the *whatever*s and the *my bad*s and the *LOL*s before you realized that he was quoting from Mao's November 15, 1956, Speech at the Second Plenum of the Eighth Central Committee of the Communist Party

of China about the suppression of counterrevolutionaries. This all came up because he'd said, relative to
our idea of nonexpository autobiography, that literary-
style anecdotes were like "little Chiang Kai-sheks," and
needed to be "executed," and I said, "What do you
mean by that?" and that's when he, in his diffident
phumphering way, quoted Mao: "They [the counterrev-
olutionaries] ought to be executed. Some of the democratic personages say that it is bad to execute [these
people]. We say that it is good to execute them; this is
just a competing show. In this drama we have always
been singing in disharmony with the democratic personages. The ones we are executing are 'little Chiang
Kai-sheks'... If the counterrevolutionaries are not sup-
pressed, the laboring people will not be happy. The oxen
will not be happy either; nor will the plows, and the soil
will not be comforted. This is because the laboring people who use the oxen, the plows, and the land are not
happy. Therefore, we must execute some counterrevolutionaries." But this all had to be painstakingly gleaned
through a translation process of which only I was capable, given the propinquity of our thought processes.

Mom, do you have any of that, uh...that, that mois-
turizer with you? The stuff with the hyaluronic acid?

*(MARK'S MOM rummages through her bag and retrieves a small
bottle of moisturizing lotion. MARK gets down from the table and takes
the bottle from her.)*

MARK

Thank you.

(He squeezes out a few daubs into the palm of his hand, and gets back up on the table.)

MARK
(To the fast-food workers.)

Y'know, when Mao says "laboring people," he means you guys.

(He massages the lotion into his wrinkled neck.)

MARK

Even in my most drunken, obstreperous state, when I'm like a thrashing, sweaty, demented infant...some frothing homunculus...one's impulse is to embrace me, to hold me in your arms, to stroke my little, balding, translucent skull and console me, "Poor Leyner...poor, poor Leyner," as one might say to some homesick alien creature or some morose ape in a tuxedo.

I think I was in maybe ninth grade, tenth grade, when I failed shop class after basically just taking a very large piece of wood and planing it down day after day until it was ultimately a very tiny piece of wood...I guess I made a toothpick. That ended up unintentionally being my final project. Other kids had made these great planters and bookends and stuff...I definitely do like cutting things into smaller and smaller pieces...Maybe it's a core aesthetic strategy of mine, come to think of it—to create a kind of plenitude, not by generating anything new, but by endlessly dividing what I originally had. Perhaps my revenge on the world as a small-statured male (I'm like five seven–ish) is to literally cut everything else down to size. The ant and the mouse (obvious personifications of my stature) have always been my totem animals. I still have an enduring identification with, uh...I don't know what you'd call them...maybe *stigmatized* animals...which is reflected in a lot of the poems I post on Twitter, e.g.,

Still looking for homes for:
Muffin, a 7-ft adult tapeworm;
Buster, a 10-month-old Ixodes tick;
& Lulu, a 4-day-old streptococcus bacterium.

So anyway, to make up the credits I lost by failing shop, I took a summer class at a community college, which was fairly close to where we lived at the time in Maplewood, New Jersey. I think it was an Intro to Classical Music survey type of thing, which seemed relatively painless. And the teacher, the professor, offered me a ride home one day, and on the way he swung by his house and offered me a beer. I said fine and went in and sat on his couch in the living room, and he came on to me. And I said, No thanks, and he told me that he'd fucked Leonard Bernstein, and that he could play me like a Stradivarius...I still think about this (and sort of wince, actually) whenever I hear a piece of music that features pizzicato, that rapid plucking of the strings...again I said, No thanks, and he was super-cool about it. I bring this all up simply to point out that, although I think now I have the face of an ogre, of some old, Belgian, morphine-dependent, defrocked priest (I have *no* idea why I said "Belgian" just now), I was sort of cute back then. But, God, how we change! We droop, we prolapse, we...we curdle and decay...we putrefy and deliquesce and melt into these foul, slimy puddles of our-selves...Unless we're somehow extracted from this evil world...somehow rescued from above.

It's a great relief, actually, after squinting at the ap-paritions of pseudocelebrities for almost six decades, to look at yourself in the mirror, to look at your own anony-mous, moribund face. In my own eyes, I can see the tiny nuns floating across the boulevard, perhaps it's just that degenerative debris that floats in the vitreous humor of the eye, but to me, it's tiny Jersey City nuns. There is something unspeakably consoling in one's own smile. In that reflection, you can discern the face of yourself as a child and the face of yourself as a corpse. And in this moment, all the fundamental antinomies are reconciled—the sacred and the profane, the analyst and

the analysand, the celebrated success and the abject failure. The pilot and the passenger. Writer and reader.
Fiction and nonfiction. Past and present. And the mind
that abides and the mind that is gone.

The Imaginary Intern and I used to watch lots of lec-
tures and documentaries on YouTube. One of our fa-
vorites was by Masakazu Konishi, a Japanese neuro-
biologist known for his research on the prey-capture
auditory systems of barn owls. There was a video we
loved about the symbiotic relationship between Hawaiian bobtail squid (*Euprymna scolopes*) and bioluminescent
bacteria called *Vibrio fischeri,* which colonize the crypts in
the squid's light organ (the benefit to the squid is that
this illumination offsets that of the moonlight so that it
doesn't cast a shadow which makes it conspicuous to
prey)...there was a video of crabs eating jellyfish go-
nads...oh, there was one depicting a feeding frenzy
of deep-sea snailfish (*Notoliparis kermadecensis*), which are
adapted to extreme pressure, total darkness, and cold
temperature, and at about the ten-second mark, this
twenty-five-centimeter giant white sea-monster crus-
tacean thing (*Alicella gigantea*) swims into the frame, and
even though we'd both watched it maybe a hundred
times, the two of us would just sit there dumbstruck!
(My old high-school friend Danny Sarewitz—who now
edits *Issues in Science and Technology,* a magazine copub-
lished by the National Academy of Sciences—told me
once that I'm an *extremophilephile.*) But sometimes I just

wanted to watch something sort of light and silly, and one night we happened on *The Expendables*, this movie starring Sylvester Stallone, Jason Statham, Jet Li, and Dolph Lundgren. And the Imaginary Intern, using one of his quainter expressions of disinclination, said, "I'd rather watch a person scoop shit out of his ass and frost a cake with it than watch *The Expendables*." And what happens of course? We watch it and he *loves* it, which is, I think, exactly what he was most apprehensive about in the first place. We most resist what we most desire. It's all an endless reenactment of the incest taboo. We also loved watching—and I almost forgot this one—the video that was recorded during a cystoscopy performed on me by my urologist, Dr. David Samadi (there's a miniature video camera on the tip of the scope). And there's a moment when Samadi gets to my bladder and this bladder stone comes into view—it looks like this little golden nugget—and the same thing would happen...even though the Imaginary Intern and I had watched this video I don't know how many times (and this is one you *really* should watch high), when that bladder stone would come into view, we'd both go fucking bonkers! I'm completely convinced that endoscopic imaging is the ne plus ultra of reality TV, and I think that once the equipment comes down in price, people will just start sticking scopes down their throats and up their asses, and just sit around and watch that all day. Duchamp spent the last two decades of his life secretly constructing this very enigmatic assemblage called *Étant donnés* in a clandestine space off the bathroom in his apartment on West Fourteenth Street, leading everyone in the art world to believe that he'd stopped working as an artist...that he'd abandoned art to devote himself to chess. With *Gone with the Mind,* the Imaginary Intern and I decided to do exactly the opposite. We made a great display of working every day, but we were actually doing nothing. Well...we were tweeting, looking at porn, playing video games (or attempting to, at any rate), watching shit on YouTube, watching old movies on TCM, etc. But we weren't "writing" per se. And he was always busting my balls about how long it was taking...he was always reminding me that Nietzsche wrote his autobiographical *Ecce Homo* in only two months as he teetered on the brink of complete syphilitic insanity, so he didn't see why it should be any problem for us to get this done by...whatever deadline we'd imposed on ourselves at that point. But if it weren't for Internet porn, I'm sure we would have finished *Gone with the Mind* a lot sooner. If it weren't for Internet porn, there'd be a cure for cancer, there'd be human photosynthesis, levitation, time travel, everything...Men spend so much time looking at Internet porn that surely they (we) will evolve into some sort of mutant creature consisting entirely of an eye, a hand, and a penis. And you know what's funny? Liz Ross, my high-school girlfriend with whom I've remained very close over the years, read a tweet I posted that said, *Yay! Candy Crush Saga has cured me of my Internet-porn addiction!* and she texted me and she didn't even mention the Internet-porn thing, all she wanted to know was what level of Candy Crush Saga I was on. (Who even plays Candy Crush anymore, right?) But just to circle back to something I was talking about before...I was thinking in the car on the way here tonight about Liz's selective attention in reading my tweet, about that sort of goal-driven selective or executive attention, which is the...the cognitive protocol, the process by which we key in on task-related stimuli (e.g., info about Candy Crush) and filter out irrelevant or distracting information or "noise" (e.g., my Internet-porn addiction)...and I was thinking about how not only has this kind of executive attention been a hallmark of Liz's cognitive style since I met her (when I was fifteen, after weeks and weeks of stirring up the courage to call and ask her out, I finally did, and she answered the phone and said, "Could you call me back, I'm watching *Upstairs, Downstairs,*" which was this British drama that took place in a town house in Edwardian London and depicted the lives of the servants "downstairs" and their masters "upstairs")...but I was also thinking about how functional magnetic resonance imaging (fMRI) has consistently shown that executive attention is mediated by the dorsal/caudal regions of the anterior cingulate cortex (also known as Area 25), and I started thinking, wouldn't *that* be the ultimate reality show? Watching an fMRI of your own anterior cingulate cortex as you watch an fMRI of your own anterior cingulate cortex? Shows like *Deadliest Catch* and *The Real Housewives of At-*

lanta can pull in, I don't know, close to four million viewers, but I just can't imagine that wouldn't be more popular. I mean...it's watching your own mind watch itself watching itself (which is another way of describing autobiography, I suppose). The Imaginary Intern and I used to say, "The mind going is the mind coming," which we meant not only in terms of the curvature of space-time (and the cosmic boomerang effect), but also in terms of sexual *jouissance*.

Finally...I just want to acknowledge and thank two people I haven't mentioned thus far who helped with the autobiography—the psychiatrist Dr. Robert Berger and the psychic Janet Horton.

Bobby Berger is a very interesting, extraordinarily smart, compassionate guy I met years ago at Bellevue Hospital in New York City, when he was the director of forensic psychiatry there. In early May of 2014, I drove up to Westport, Connecticut, to visit him and talk about *Gone with the Mind*. (He currently works for the Correctional Managed Health Care Division of UConn Health, which provides medical and mental-health services for the jails and prisons of Connecticut.) He and his wife and son live in a wonderful old house up there with a rambunctiously affectionate French bulldog named Dot. We sat down in his office, I drank black coffee, he smoked Camels. I began talking to him about my original conception for *Gone with the Mind*—the first-person shooter game involving Mussolini's flying balcony, fighting your way backwards through my life until getting into my mother's uterus and unraveling the zygote. Berger understood instinctively that this, far from representing any kind of suicidal imperative, signified the intention to return home, to a pre-individuated existence, a world before man, to rid oneself of one's self, to truly become something else, etc. We chatted about video games a bit, and I told him about how I'd found it impossible to get beyond even the most rudimentary level of Call of Duty and quickly became demoralized and bored with it all. Then I showed him a photo on my phone of the bathroom tiles with the craquelure suggesting the lineaments, the face of the Imaginary Intern, and I got the feeling that he was a little, I don't know, a little skeptical about his existence, and I said, "Y'know, it's funny, it was actually the Imaginary Intern who suggested I talk to you in the first place!" (He showed me a photo of him and his wife, Linda, dressed as Andy Warhol and Edie Sedgwick for a Halloween party.) I explained how the book in its original conception began to seem like this tedious obligation to me and how the Imaginary Intern helped me reconceptualize it, how we wanted to create an autobiography that is a record of its own making, that hides nothing, but rather renders its mode of production transparent—*prozrachnost*. I don't remember if I showed him a picture of her or not, but I certainly discussed with him how much I'd been thinking about the Russian constructivist Varvara Stepanova. Berger grinned at me. "You're into her. You have a crush on her, don't you?" Even though Stepanova died in 1958 (or perhaps *because* she had), I blushed, making it obvious that, yes, I did have a crush on her. I explained the book's protagonist—an angry, moribund man who, on the inside, is a sleepy little boy wandering around the piazza in his pajamas, holding a balloon on a string, who, more than anything else, just wants everyone in the world to like him, etc. It was difficult describing the project to him because it seemed to me at the time so abstract and inchoate. But he easily assimilated it all and seemed to get it completely. "Something about what you were saying before about your fascination with cyborgs and the surgical robot who removed your prostate gave me an idea," he said. He got a booklet out of a folder. "This is the Minnesota Multiphasic Personality Inventory. It's a standardized psychometric test we use to assess and analyze an individual's personality dynamic. It's got about six hundred true-or-false questions. You fill this out and then the computer will generate a report." Well, I thought this was absolutely perfect! I was just delighted with the idea that psychodiagnostic algorithms would generate a posthumanist psychiatric profile of me for the autobiography. And both the Imaginary Intern and I felt this would really streamline the process, that it would save us a tremendous amount of work, and obviate the need for all that cloying introspection and redemptive candor that we both found so nauseating and counterrevolutionary.

So, I just want to read several excerpts from this interpretive report...

(MARK crouches down, opens an old nylon messenger bag on the table, and thumbs through a miscellany of papers.)

MARK

Fuck...

(He flips through the sheaf of papers once again, shaking his head in consternation.)

MARK

Well...unfortunately...

MARK'S MOM

I've got it.

(She reaches into her handbag and retrieves the MMPI-2 report.)

MARK'S MOM

Would you like me to just read it?

MARK

Sure.

MARK'S MOM

The whole thing?

MARK

Just read the highlighted sections, please.

MARK'S MOM
(Skimming through the report.)

The highlighted sections...the highlighted sections...
okay:

(She clears her throat.)

"He endorsed a number of unusual, bizarre ideas
that—"

MARK

Mom...first, could you just read the test date on the, uh...on the cover page, and then the ID number, which, if I remember correctly, is on the upper right-hand corner of each ensuing page...I just want to establish the authenticity of the document.

MARK'S MOM

The test date is May 7, 2014. And the ID number is, um...let's see...upper right-hand corner...okay...the ID number is 654321.

MARK

Thank you. Now the highlighted sections, if you would...

MARK'S MOM

"He endorsed a number of unusual, bizarre ideas that suggest some difficulties with his thinking...He may physically or verbally attack others when he is angry...He is likely to be considered by others as a pervasively aggressive person...[He] apparently holds some unusual beliefs that suggest he may be somewhat disconnected from reality...and might experience unusual symptoms such as delusional beliefs, circumstantial and tangential thinking, and loosening of associations...He feels intensely angry, hostile, and resentful of others, and he would like to get back at them...He may be visibly uneasy around others, sits alone in group situations...his unusual thinking and bizarre ideas need to be taken into consideration in any diagnostic formulation...His acknowledged problems with alcohol and drug use should be addressed in therapy."

(MARK folds his arms across his chest, juts out his chin, and surveys the food court.)

MARK

I don't come here tonight as a panegyrist of my own bowel movements, believe me. That's what mothers are for. Thank you, Mom.

I just have one comment about the report. I believe that I have a genetic predisposition to violence and narcissistic acting-out. This is essentially what my mother was corroborating in her introduction earlier when, describing my first birthday party, she said, "He received beautiful gifts, put both fists in the cake, cried at the company, and later in the evening 'performed' for them and for the camera." I believe that I inherited my predisposition to violence from my mother who, again, in her introduction, admitted first to assaulting her aunt Bea: "That summer, I was really acting out, I know I was...I remember I slapped my aunt Beatrice across the face. That's the thing I remember the most that shows how completely wacko I was. She was an overbearing person and bossy, and she said something to me that I didn't take well, and instead of just telling her to mind her own business or whatever, I just reached over and gave her a good one across the face." And then, when she was talking about that anti-Semitic nurse at the hospital, admitted, "I walked toward her, as I remember, one or two steps, because I really wanted to just do something horrible to her."

"I really wanted to just do something horrible to her."

I think it's pretty clear where I get all this from.

I have a friend by the name of Eugene Flynn. Eugene owns several very successful restaurants in Hoboken: Amanda's, the Café Elysian, and Schnackenberg's Luncheonette. My father is forever telling me what a savvy businessman Eugene is, how lucrative his restaurants are, and how everything he touches seems to turn to gold (in contrast to yours truly here). And one night I was sitting at Amanda's having dinner with my mom. We were having a long convoluted argument about something...about this stupid incident involving a sister-in-law and a piece of furniture...I'm not going to get into it here. It's rare that my mom and I ever have arguments of any kind, rarer still that they ever get as heated as this one did.

And at one point, she said to me, "You look just like your father right now."

And I was like: "Did I ask you to fuck the guy and make me?"

At that very moment, Eugene, who was sitting with some of his employees on a banquette at the back of the room...my mom and I were the last table, and they were all waiting for us to finish so they could get out of there...Eugene, just kidding around, flung a wet tea bag at me, and it hit me with a very audible *splat!* right on the bald spot on top of my head. And because I was in such a particularly foul, irascible mood, I got up and walked over to King Midas over there and swung as hard as I could and punched him in the head. Thankfully he flinched at the last second, so it ended up just being a sort of glancing shot off the top of his forehead. And I immediately felt enormously remorseful and ashamed— it was really such an awful, reprehensible thing to do (and to a friend yet!)—and Eugene immediately forgave me, because...because Eugene is such a sweet, decent person. He really really is. But none of this would have happened if I didn't have a genetic predisposition for violence and my father would just stop always reminding me how much money Eugene makes. Unlike a mother and a son, who frequently eschew spoken language in favor of telepathy, a father and son can engage in endless viva voce banter, endless glib small talk about money, jobs, real estate, etc. It's the sort of reassuring, inoffensive repartee that enables most men to endure—enjoy, even—their stultifying lives of shit-eating servitude. Unlike this casual copraphagia, though, and in the way a bird passes a kind of premasticated ambrosia from her mouth to the mouths of her chicks, mothers try to nourish their sons for extra-ordinary lives of heroism and martyrdom.

There was a golden age for me when it was just my mother and myself, and this is still the idealized world I long for, still the mythic, primordial time, the paradisiacal status quo ante that I persistently hearken back to, whose restoration is at the core of a mystico-fascistic politics. The world that my mother and I created for ourselves was very refined, and I always thought of everything that lay beyond it as a kind of oceanic sewer. And when I realized that it was no longer possible to maintain the purity, the, uh...the exclusivity of that sublime world, it was...it was very difficult for me...for a very long time. I loved poetry, but suddenly the only poems that interested me anymore were the ingredient lists on cans of dog food and the litany of side effects in pharmaceutical ads. It was as if a witch man from the netherworld was magically eating my in-sides. Finally, one afternoon, I drank an entire bottle of Novahistine Elixir and melted, one by one, a boxful of my most prized crayons (the ones reserved for my jet-fighter drawings) in the hot steam that issued continuously from the vaporizer in my bedroom—a young valetudinarian's rite of passage. Then I tried to melt my plastic Civil War soldiers. Would you believe that, after all those years, I still have several of the more grotesquely misshapen ones that I keep in a jar?

But my mother and I have preserved our beautiful closeness. And I think at this stage in our lives, we're happiest when we're able to descant upon our grievances and the grave injustices to which we've been subjected, happiest when we're reenacting some tragic event, some traumatic iniquity...something that is for us like the Battle of Karbala is for Shia Muslims or like the Battle of Kosovo in 1389 is for the Serbians.

It's so obvious to me that the fact that I'm going to be reading my book at the food court tonight is meant to evoke the "eating books" of my childhood that my mother spoke about—those books like *The Tawny Scrawny Lion* or *The Musicians of Bremen* that she'd read to me as I ate...and I guess I was hoping that *Gone with the Mind* might, here at this food court, perhaps become the "eating book" of some other withdrawn, delicate, mother-fixated boy...but since you guys don't seem to me particularly withdrawn, delicate, or mother-fixated—

(The fast-food workers don't react in any way to this.)

MARK

And I also think that reading here at this food court is an homage, a kind of...uh...a kind of ceremonial re-enactment of those lunches at the Bird Cage at Lord & Taylor that my mom and I used to enjoy, just the two of us, talking and talking...first my mom, and I'd sit there and listen so intently, and then me, and she'd listen and smile...just like tonight, here. You know...in Shakespeare's play, King Lear says to his daughter Cordelia: "Come, let's away to prison. / We two alone will sing like birds i' th' cage. / When thou dost ask me blessing, I'll kneel down / And ask of thee forgiveness. So we'll live, / And pray, and sing, and tell old tales, and laugh / At gilded butterflies." Isn't that just amazing?! We two alone like birds i' th' cage? That's my mom and me at the Bird Cage at Lord & Taylor! I mean, c'mon, right? Telling old tales and laughing at gilded butterflies! Right?

Armin Meiwes was a forty-two-year-old computer expert from a small German town called Rotenburg who, in 2001, posted an advertisement on the website the Cannibal Café stating that he was "looking for a well-built eighteen- to thirty-year-old to be slaughtered and then consumed." Bernd Jurgen Armando Brandes, an engineer from Berlin, answered the notice, and was then, as advertised, slaughtered and consumed by Meiwes.

I really think this kind of consensual cannibalism is such a perfect analogue for the reciprocal relationship between writer and reader, and especially between writers and readers of autobiography. The reader of an autobiography consumes the life of the author, and the author, in turn, consumes the life of the reader, that portion of it surrendered to reading, or listening to, the autobiography.

And you have to admit that it's pretty interesting that, given all the uncanny correspondences between auto-biography and cannibalism, that this reading is taking place at a *food* court, and that the audience for my work, for the most part, tends to be well built and between eighteen and thirty years old. Granted, it's a dwindling audience, if the fact that only two people showed up tonight for my reading is any indication...

PANDA EXPRESS WORKER

For the hundred and fiftieth fucking time, we are *not* here for the reading. We're on break, dickwad.

(MARK smiles sweetly at him.)

MARK

Sometimes I'll stop on the sidewalk to text or tweet something on my phone, and then I'll finish and look up and—for a moment—I won't know where I am or even how old I am. If I feel the hot sun on the back of my neck, I'll think I'm nine and I'm back at summer camp in the Adirondacks. I'm back with that red-haired counselor from Alabama who told me that I was his favorite in the entire bunk, the only "mature" one, and promised to visit me someday at home and take me to the movies.

(He did: *Yellow Submarine.*) And then I'll sort of snap out of it and realize, *Oh, I'm standing here on the street in Hobo-ken. I'm fifty-eight.* And I'll wonder for a second, *What's the matter with me? Did getting hit in the head with that tea bag ex-acerbate my chronic traumatic encephalopathy? Do I have a brain tumor or something?* Because my mom had a brain tumor, a benign tumor, something called a hemangioblastoma, which she had removed at Mount Sinai Hospital. Thank God it was a completely successful operation, she made a full recovery with no repercussions, no neuropsycho-logical consequences at all. But it was a very tense, very grim moment as they were about to wheel her off to surgery, and I said to the surgeon, I guess to try and lighten the mood a little...I said to him, "Y'know, as long as you're gonna be poking around in there, in her brain, can you see if there's anything you can do about how much she talks? I think there might be a switch in there that's stuck in the on position or something." And a couple of months after her surgery, to celebrate, I took my mom out to dinner at Raoul's in SoHo in New York City, and she asked the waiter if there was a discount on the caviar for people who've recently had brain tumors. And the waiter said, "Let me check." Isn't that fantastic? "Let me check." First of all, it's a wonderful question with far-reaching implications. My mother is from the you-don't-know-until-you-ask gen-eration which believes that people languish in life not because of socioeconomic barriers, but because they are too coy, because they leave the world inadequately interrogated. I also think my mom "suffers" from something one might call Pollyanna's paranoia, an irrational suspicion that there are people out there secretly trying to do *good* things to you, that there are all sorts of hidden perks lurking everywhere, almost like the Easter eggs in video games... that it's possible that Raoul's might be running some sort of unpublicized hemangioblastoma-all-the-caviar-you-can-eat promotion. (I'm from the never-ask-anything school. I'll never forget cringing with mortification when my dad asked for coarse-cut Seville marmalade at a fucking Denny's in Nebraska. I mean, would you ask for an ortolan drowned in Armagnac at KFC? I suppose it can't hurt, right?) Well, the waiter came back from the kitchen and informed us that, no, there wasn't such a caviar discount, and he seemed genuinely indignant about it, and he did bring us extra toast points, I remember—it was sort of all-the-toast-points-you-can-eat actually, which earned him an enormous tip, because people just love it when they think a service employee is playing some double game, that he or she has turned against the house and is now allied with you to procure illicit little freebies, even if it's just extra toast points. Why would we not only believe, but become eternally beholden to some unctuous car salesman who claims to be putting the lives of his own children at risk by throwing in floor mats and a bug deflector? (I know why *I* would—because I'm so emotionally gullible, so desperate for tiny kindnesses in my misery.)

At Raoul's there's a spiral staircase next to the bar

that runs upstairs to where the bathrooms are located. And up on that second floor, they traditionally host a psychic who does tarot card readings, and the resident psychic at Raoul's at the time that my mother and I were celebrating her successful brain surgery was a woman named Janet Horton (whom the Imaginary Intern and I would dub simply Janet the Psychic). I didn't know Janet the Psychic back then because I never got a tarot reading at Raoul's. I'd just go up to the second floor, pee, and come back down again, which does seem to represent a very common kind of unexamined life, doesn't it?—drinking and urinating and drinking and urinating, without ever pausing to ascertain what the future might hold in store. But I would meet her several years later, because it turns out that, with great literary serendipity, Janet the Psychic lives in Hoboken and works out at the same gym as I do, the New York Sports Club on Fourteenth Street.

In the spring of, uh, 2014, I went over to Janet the Psychic's exceptionally tidy apartment in Hoboken, and she did a tarot card reading for me...and I remember there were two beautiful trees in front of her building, a honey locust and a ginkgo with its veiny fan-shaped leaves and its stinky fruit, its stinky nuts, and there was one of those grotesque little drug-addled mercenaries in Heidi braids and thick cat's-eye glasses patrolling the sidewalk on her Huffy Disney Princess bike with pink streamers on the handlebars...and I could hear her through Janet's open

window, and the Doppler effect of her bell was the ob-
bligato of the entire reading.

The most interesting thing Janet revealed had absolutely nothing to do with me. Before she started my
reading, she told me a marvelous story about contacting
the spirit of a man's dead hamster. The man had apparently been extraordinarily close to this hamster, and I
think he felt guilty about perhaps not having taken suf-
ficiently good care of the hamster when it was ill. Janet
shuffled her tarot deck, closed her eyes, asked the hamster's spirit how it felt about the man, and dealt the cards
out onto the table.

"Your hamster thought you were a god," she told
him, once she'd had a moment to interpret the spread.

As you might suspect, I was extraordinarily moved
by this story. It would be wonderful, I thought, to be
worshipped by a hamster. I just immediately imagined,
of course, a piazza full of swooning anthropomorphic
hamsters, singing "To Sir with Love" to me. Or perhaps,
instead of a thronged piazza, there are only two anthropomorphic hamsters, just sort of loitering out on the
periphery of the piazza, "on break," indifferent…

I'm not skeptical in the least about tarot card readings.
I am very superstitious myself. I won't leave forks in the
dish rack overnight because I believe that the tines at-
tract demonic energy. If I'm at a sandwich shop like a
Subway or a Quiznos, I believe it's very bad luck to
watch the person wrap your sandwich, and I shut my

eyes or actually turn my back. And I know when I'm about to have a clairvoyant "vision" of my own—I get a little gassy and the tinea versicolor rash on my back starts to itch. Kestrels can see the UV reflection of the urine trails of the moles they hunt, so who's to gainsay what psychics claim to see? The world is endlessly generating signs, it's in perpetual blossom. Ask a question, deal the cards, and interpret. I have absolutely no problem with that at all.

You have no idea how many hours, days, weeks, months in aggregate I spend just chewing gum and sullenly throwing a pink rubber ball against a concrete abutment, and imagining random successions of things...

- Persephone weaving a great tapestry of the universe...
- A hungover Johnny Knoxville in the lobby of the Mercer Hotel...
- A father, in a sweat-drenched gray T-shirt, sprinting and propelling a jogging stroller at great speed. Child in stroller—white-knuckled grip on handles, flesh on his face rippling grotesquely like a g-force test pilot...
- A parent telling his rambunctious eight-year-old son that if he doesn't start behaving himself, he'll be transferred to Saudi intelligence, where guards rip the skin off their prisoners...
- Jimmy Kimmel trying to feed a dead mouse to an owl...

- Josephine the Singer, in Norwegian black-metal corpse paint, singing "I've Gotta Get a Message to You" on *The Voice*...
- Gucci Mane's "Lemonade" blasting from a Bose SoundDock on a night table next to a bed...
- A hawk with a kitten in its mouth flying over the Staples Center...
- Regurgitated yarn...
- A bleached-blond woman in her mid-fifties struggling with a wheelchair in the trunk of her Civic. Her severely brain-damaged adult son sits in the front seat of the car, spastically wrenching his head from side to side. A small dog yelps in the backseat. "Shut up," she says flatly, squinting through cigarette smoke. She rolls her son in the wheelchair perilously close to the edge of the pier. It's impossible to tell if he's elated or terrified as he gapes at the river, ablaze with sunlight. The hollow, breaking voices of adolescent boys, flinging chunks of concrete and scrap rebar into the water, resound in the near distance...
- A motorcyclist slapping a magnetized bomb on the side of a car...
- Superman squeezing a lump of coal in his closed hand until it becomes a diamond...
- A professor, using only items purchased from a gas-station vending machine, reconstructs the genome of an extinct mammal...
- Along the periphery of a multiplex parking lot, a

group of hermits, fugitive serfs, brigands, mystics, and lost children emerging from the forest...

- Surgical robots going wild and stalking the country-side, tearing out men's prostates...
- My mind disappearing, leaving behind a trail of thought bubbles...azure thought bubbles that are indistinguishable from the sky...

...and yet these things, these random elements in this "montage," are trying to form a sentence, don't you think?...A...a sort of rebus...as surely as the Queen of Wands, the Ace of Pentacles, the Knight of Cups in reverse, and the Chariot cards dealt out on the table of a psychic are trying to articulate something...

It is as impossible not to see a sort of inchoate matrix of meaning forming in these...these little random scenarios...these little random private memes...as it is not to see a face in the cracks across a bathroom tile. There's a sort of immediate time-lapse ramifying interweaving of meaning that goes on...a putting out of shoots...these little ramifying filamentous tendrils of correlation...or something like the configuration of iron filings in a magnetic field.

So, just as we read the world, the encrypted world, in all its efflorescing glory, with all its bristling signification, with all its bulk metadata to analyze and interpret...Janet dealt her cards and surveyed the spread, and interpreted them...and I'm going to get into all this later in greater detail of course, but here are some quick highlights:

- "God and the spirits are saying, 'You're unhappy.'"

I assumed this was referring to my "misery," to the modern condition of exile and deracination, of paradises lost. Of being forced to curry favor with white Western intellectuals in a milieu of capitalist consumerism.

- "Whatever you're working on now, however much you might be struggling, and thinking, *Am I doing it right?* ... Yeah ... you're doing it absolutely brilliantly."

I gave a fist pump to the Imaginary Intern (wherever he is now).

- "Are you cancer-free or will you have a recurrence in the future? Pick five."

I chose five cards from the deck. Janet scrutinized them carefully, brow knit, biting her lip ...

"It looks like it's totally over. But you continue to worry about it—who wouldn't? What you worry about, you create. That was brave for us to ask that question."

Us? I thought. That sort of reminded me of something my mom once told me (re: her brain tumor, my cancer, and how glib even the most well-meaning people can be commiserating with you), "Whenever anyone says to you, 'We'll get through this together,' what they really mean is 'God, am I glad it isn't me.'"

- "What do God and the spirits want you to know about your doctor, Dr. Samadi? Pick five."

Again, I chose five cards. Janet appraised them for a moment or two and chuckled.

"Has your wife spent any time with Dr. Samadi?"

"Mercedes? Aside from a few minutes right after my prostatectomy, no."

She gave the cards another perusal.

"Well, I think on a visceral level your urologist thought your wife was a very attractive lady, because it comes up twice that way. He finds her *very* attractive."

(I had dinner with Mercedes that night at the Café Elysian [one of Eugene Flynn's restaurants], and I told her about what Janet Horton had said, and she was sort of like, "I *wish*…" reminding me of a recent *New York Post* article proclaiming Samadi the highest-paid hospital-based physician in New York City, raking in $7.6 million.) There are two major potential side effects of a radical prostatectomy: urinary incontinence and impotence. My dad, who was vehemently opposed to the surgery (he's partial to proton-beam radiation therapy), had tried to gently dissuade me by suggesting that Mercedes would leave me if the prostatectomy left me impotent. It all made me think about what an incredibly cruel joke it would be if your urologist, who's essentially the lord of your penis, were having an affair with your wife…it would be like some…some modern, biopolitical version of droit du seigneur, wouldn't it? Or if there were a club or a...a *cabal* of evil urologists gelding their patients and seducing their wives. But, to get back to reality here, back to nonfiction...David Samadi is probably the top robotic radical prostatectomy surgeon in the world...I would say he's like the, uh...the Alexander Ovechkin of robotic radical prostatectomy surgery...and, just on a purely personal level, I think, an extraordinarily caring person. And if either of you guys ever need a prostatectomy, this is your guy. I'd be more than happy to give him a call.

• Janet contacted each of my deceased grandparents:

   Ray: You're doing a great job of looking after your Mom. I really appreciate that.

   Sam: You've done a great job as a dad.

   Harriet: You're not having enough happy-go-lucky sex.

   Rose: Have sex, have fun. Life will get you in the end, so enjoy it.

The obvious implication here is that your dead grandparents are watching you fuck. Again, this is probably something the government knows and is suppressing.

*   *   *

Several weeks after the reading, I realized that I'd neglected to ask Janet to contact my deceased sister. I asked her if it would be possible to have a "conversation" with the spirit of someone who'd only survived a week or so, and Janet explained to me that spirits age on the other side and that, yes, it was a perfectly feasible thing to try, and we made arrangements to do it over the phone.

A couple of highlights:

- "You're my darling brother. Your sister is also my beloved...I'm still here and there are things you need to know. And I can be more released after this." (Janet interjected at this point: "She's a spirit in an adult state, I'd say in her mid-thirties, married. She feels French to me, as opposed to Jewish or American...maybe French in a past life.")

- "Give your father an easier time, he's not going to be around forever. Enjoy him while he's here."

(I really took this to heart. I do tend to be very impatient with my father. I was out to dinner with him the other night and I was telling him about Liz's response to my tweet *Yay! Candy Crush Saga has cured me of my Internet-porn addiction!* in which she didn't even mention the Internet-porn thing and just wanted to know what level of Candy Crush Saga I was on, and he just did not understand what was funny about that. And after repeating it to him, more slowly with each iteration, which, I know, in itself, probably felt condescending to him, I tried to come up with some analogous scenario that he might understand...I said, "Okay, Dad, what if you're playing tennis with someone"—my father loves tennis—"and you get a call that your son was just killed in a...by a bomb, okay? And you call up a friend and you tell him, and your friend's response is 'So what's the score of your tennis match?' You don't think that would be funny?...I mean in a sort of dark way, but funny?" And he *still* didn't get it. And I really became sort of exasperated with him, and I could see that his feelings were hurt, that he thought I thought he was being stupid...It's something I absolutely need to modify...being so hard on him, so intolerant.)

- "I was there when Samadi saved you in the hospital! That's why you're still here. You had a star for a surgeon."

- Janet asked: "Is there anything we can do for you?" "No...I'm dead."

After we got off the phone, Janet texted me a photo of the Six of Cups card with the message: *Here's the Six of Cups, which represents happy children and a happy childhood. This card kept coming up for you and your sister who passed. She's around in connection with flowers. Pull up a chair and talk to her once in a while.*

This is a girl who died at one week old in a Jersey

City hospital in 1961, almost fifty-five years ago, who's now supposedly in her thirties, living in the spirit realm, living "in glory" (according to Janet), and...I don't know...it's hard after all this time to suddenly feel close to her, to just "pull up a chair"...I sort of feel that her spirit is far away...perhaps as far as thirty billion light-years away...And I think that the farther away a spirit is, the faster it is retreating from us, measured by the redshift of its light being broadened to larger wavelengths...But I told Janet I'd try to be more, uh...more receptive to her.

A few moments later, Janet texted: *Daisies especially.*

And then a few moments after that: *Turn on TCM! Child dying in hospital bed, nurse trying to save him, 1940 movie called* Vigil in the Night...*Nurse isn't attending, he passes away.*

So my deceased sister is speaking to us through daisies and Turner Classic Movies? I texted. (That sounds sarcastic, but it wasn't meant that way at all. I firmly believe that the world is constantly producing signs for us to decipher. And I was happy...I was proud of Janet, actually...that she was reading phenomena instead of simply relying on cards. The world's phenomena are just an infinite tarot deck, Janet.)

In retrospect, I was really struck—sort of offended, to be honest—by how garrulous, how indiscreet spirits can be. Apparently, there's no code of *omertà* in effect here.

So, I want to say something to all my dead relatives, particularly my grandparents:

Snitches get stitches. Keep your motherfucking mouths shut.

To Ray, Sam, Harriet, Rose—just because some psychic or medium contacts you in the afterworld, homie, that doesn't mean you have to spill your guts and start blabbing all over the place about who's having "happy-go-lucky sex" and who isn't, you know what I'm saying? Seriously. Represent.

For some reason I was reluctant to talk to Janet about the Imaginary Intern...I don't know...maybe I thought she'd think I was weird or that it would require too involved an explanation or that perhaps she couldn't contact someone or something like that...I don't know...which is funny because here's a woman who told me unabashedly and without the slightest compunction that she'd contacted the spirit of a dead hamster, right? But it ultimately just didn't feel right to me. I decided that trying to contact a paracosmic being through a psychic would just be terribly intrusive, sort of like bursting into someone's apartment with a SWAT team using C-4 explosives and battering rams. So I just let it rest.

Yes, sometimes the Imaginary Intern was like a mentor and a tutelary figure to me, but a lot of the time he was much more like a little brother...and I need to love him and care for him as much, if not more, in his absence than I did in his presence.

* * *

My mom looked up at the TV over the bar last night (I was in the middle of telling her that I might want to go out to California and grow coca...or do some...some illegal gold mining or something...anything to try to make some fucking money)...and she looked up at the TV and, recognizing his big, blowsy body, said, "Isn't that CC Sabathia?"

This was a sign too. A marvelous lightning flash. A great alphabet-soup enema that dislodged a whole impacted mass of tedious treacly anecdotes from the autobiography. My mom's unexpected recognition of CC Sabathia at the bar set off a wild ricocheting of my mind's eyeball, and served as an anticoagulant to the end of *Gone with the Mind,* constituting an astonishing victory over the forces of "storytelling," the decadent pastime of white-guard counterrevolutionaries. And this is exactly the sort of thing that keeps the mythic ur-fire of my childhood vaporizer banked forever.

Once Samadi and I were having a drink at the bar at the Four Seasons Hotel up on Fifty-Seventh Street near his old office, and he was saying to me, "You know, once they're diagnosed with cancer, they forget about the blueberries and come to me," referring, I think, to men who, when contemplating cancer in the abstract, are willing to consider all sorts of alternative-treatment modalities, but when actually diagnosed with the actual disease in their actual bodies, want the fucking cavalry called in.

Samadi's a very interesting guy, with a very, uh...Dickensian biography. He was born and raised in the Persian Jewish community of Iran and then after the revolution, when he was only fifteen years old, moved to London with his little brother, just the two of them, completely on their own. When I met him, he was the vice chair of the department of urology, and the chief of robotics and minimally invasive surgery at Mount Sinai. And now he's...he's at Lenox Hill Hospital, where he's the chair of urology and the chief of robotic surgery.

In 2012 sometime—I don't remember the month— I was diagnosed with high-grade, capsule-contained, Gleason 7 prostate cancer. And I pretty much knew from the moment I first sat down in his exam room and we discussed my situation that I wanted him to perform the surgery. Of course I got a second opinion. I went down to Johns Hopkins and consulted with a very renowned urologist down there. (This is an episode that my mom and I have entitled "Finger-Banged in Baltimore.") In addition to the eminent urologist, there seemed to be a veritable chorus line of interns, half a dozen eager young men lined up, snapping on their latex gloves, waiting to stick their fingers up my ass...it was like being in some sort of sick Busby Berkeley routine with a...a Giorgio Moroder sound track.

All the urologists I've ever met exude a certain morbid élan. After all, their beau geste is the digital rectal exam (DRE). (I became so accustomed to the procedure that once I reflexively dropped my pants and bent over at the dentist's office. The hygienist looked at me, like, "Dude, it's just a cleaning.")

But with Samadi, there's a flamboyance, a swaggering fighter-pilot sort of bravado, that I responded to very keenly. He really does possess this imperturbable aplomb and a kind of...I don't know any other way to describe it...a kind of star quality that inspires absolute confidence. We're there at the Four Seasons, at the bar, and he's explaining the anatomy to me, how the prostate is embedded within various crucial nerves that control urinary continence and erectile function, and he's joking with me that God put the prostate in such a difficult place in order to make it even harder for Samadi—to challenge his virtuosity. But he said that he, Samadi, was like Tom Cruise in that scene in *Mission Impossible* where, y'know, the guy's dangling in midair by the two wires and, without triggering any of the laser sensors, hacks into the CIA computer...in other words, he stealthily enters the body, deftly, delicately removes the prostate, and gets out, without so much as even grazing a single nerve, leaving you in full possession of your manhood and your dignity.

I was so inspired by what he was saying, by his zeal, his steely self-possession, his...his sangfroid, that—and I'm not being facetious here—I suggested we just go into the men's room and that he remove my prostate right then and there. *That's* how charismatic he is. *That's* the complete, absolute let's-do-this allegiance he instills in his patients. (Granted I had several cocktails in me.)

I remember thinking to myself, at Mount Sinai, just as

they administered the anesthesia, *If you end up incontinent and impotent, don't be a baby, deal with it*... and then laughing, *That would actually make you a baby* (I mean, those are pretty much the two key characteristics of a baby), and then waking up in what felt like an instant, in enormous pain and with a catheter stuck in my dick and, like, five big holes in my belly, like some innocent bystander in a drive-by. But the good news was (and I wouldn't know this for sure for a while) that I'm neither incontinent nor impotent. And all praise, all glory goes to David Samadi.

I was extremely—*fanatically*—devoted to doing my Kegel exercises, which one does postsurgery to ensure full restoration of urinary continence. I put my gym-rat instincts, honed over the course of a lifetime, to good use here. I did those Kegels a dozen times a day, counted them off on a set of orange prayer beads that I bought just for that purpose. I *still* do them—a set in the morning and a set before I go to sleep at night. And I now have—and I say this with a complete lack of humility—*the* strongest urinary sphincter muscles in the world. I think they will long outlive the rest of my body. In fact...you know how people say that cockroaches will survive the nuclear Armageddon? I think cockroaches *and* my urinary sphincter will survive the nuclear Armageddon. And I think that, at some point, the cockroaches will ask my urinary sphincter to be their leader. (I guess this is my own version of Manson's Helter Skelter scenario.)

Because of what he did for me, I've got David Samadi's back for life. I consider him my homeboy. And I consider his robot my homeboy too.

When old Yurok Indians get sick, eels, along with acorn soup and seaweed, are the food they crave. When I returned home from the hospital, I wanted Peeps and Peanut M&M's, cocktail weenies and marzipan. But I was only allowed clear liquids at first, and then soft food, pabulum.

Is there a less virile look to present to one's wife than an open plaid robe, a catheterized penis, and a urine-collection bag taped to your thigh? What can you do with this? I mean, fashion-wise? Tape the bag at a sort of rakish angle? I would look in the mirror at myself and think: *This must be the most abject, undignified, de-eroticized version of a man possible.* If I were ever asked by some young, sensitive writer just starting out, what key lesson I've learned in life (which I'll never be), I'd probably say that there is no aperture of egress, however tiny and exquisitely sensitive, that can't be turned into an aperture of ingress.

I should read you the instructions they gave me at the hospital…There were like twenty-three pages of instructions…it was like a fucking novel…Take one Cipro two times a day, one Colace every eight hours, fifty milligrams of Lopressor two times a day, one oxycodone every four hours, plus applying antibiotic and lidocaine to the "entry site" of the catheter, rinsing the urine-collection bags, repositioning the taping of the catheter and the bag (to prevent blistering), what to do if you experience abdominal distension, bladder spasms, bloody drainage, ankle swelling, perineal discomfort, scrotal swelling, painful sneezing, what to eat until you pass gas, what to eat once you have passed gas, etc., when to call to get the results of the pathology report about whether there's additional cancer in surrounding tissue, when to call to schedule the removal of the catheter...I should read some of this to you...seriously...Mom, you didn't bring that too, did you? My discharge packet from Mount Sinai? No?

Anyway...Mercedes would bring me scrambled eggs and toast, or macaroni and cheese, or just pastina with butter, or whatever...and she would have made exactly the same thing for herself, so I wouldn't be envious of what she was eating...And I'd say, You don't have to do this, y'know—sit here with me and eat, it couldn't be all that appetizing. And she'd say, I want to. And when we were finished eating she would lie next to me, my catheter trailing down the side of the bed into that bag that I'd lay on the floor...and she'd hold my hand. And I don't think I ever felt more loved than at that very moment. It was just the most wonderful thing. Isn't it crazy that when I was in this abject, humiliating state, somehow that week was a kind of honeymoon? Really. Like a kind of honeymoon in Paris or something...It was.

If I were to make a coat of arms, an escutcheon...or perhaps a new tarot card...to represent love, to represent caring...it would feature a catheter, a dish of scrambled eggs, and clasped hands...

It was just the most beautiful thing anyone had ever done for me...it was the most romantic thing in the world...For Mercedes...this sweet, sweet person...to hold out her hand to me like that...It was just the most...it was the happiest moment of my life—

MARK'S MOM

Okay, *that's* enough...I mean, if we're going to have any time for questions, for the Q and A.

(MARK'S MOM is putting on lipstick, fishing car keys from her bag, ready to go.

MARK gives her a...a sort of beseeching look, and then sighs.)

MARK

In the words of the great Maximilien Robespierre, "I no longer have the strength to battle the aristocracy's intrigues."

(He bows deeply.)

Dōmo arigatō.

PART III

Q&A

(MARK gets down from the table. He notices that both his shoes are untied [they're brand-new shoes his mother bought him especially for the reading, and they've got those slippery, waxy laces that tend to unknot themselves], and he bends down to tie them.

And when he stands upright again and looks around, his mom is gone.

Gone.

He reconnoiters the entirety of the food court, his eyes panning rapidly back and forth as he weaves around the tables and banquettes, and paces several times around the circumference of fast-food franchises—past the Popeyes, Hawaiian Grill, Taste of India, Burger King, Taco Bell, Johnny Rockets, Red Mango, Subway...

But she's nowhere to be found.

The PANDA EXPRESS and SBARRO workers have also vanished.

*The disappearance of his mother immediately triggers a state of acute
panic. His pulse thrumming in his ears, a flood of gruesome thoughts
and premonitions fills his head.*

*He embarks upon a frantic, redundant search of the adjoining areas of
the empty mall, descending the motionless escalator, striding past the You
Are Here directory, past the lobby of the AMC multiplex, past the
Limited, Clarks, f.y.e., Vans, Macy's, Foot Locker, Kohl's, Sears, JC
Penney, Sunglass Hut, Bath & Body Works, Sephora, past a threading
station, and an electronic-cigarette and tongue-ring kiosk, and then
bounding back up the inert escalator several steps at a time, reprising the
search of the food court, and then back down the escalator and past the
very same stores and the very same kiosks yet again . . . like those looping,
wraparound backgrounds in early video games . . . until finally, through a
corridor of gumball machines, he reaches the restrooms, which somehow
he'd failed to notice the first time around.*

*Trembling, his heart pounding in his chest, he knocks on the door to the
ladies' room.*

There's no response.

He knocks again, harder, more insistently.)

Q. Mom, are you in here?

A. Yes.

216

Q. Are you okay?

A. Yes.

Q. Mom, I've been looking all over for you! I was *so* worried...I was going crazy.

A. Oh, sweetheart, I'm sorry. You really need to come in here. I have to show you something.

(He stretches his neck, which is clenched tight with tension, takes a deep breath, and lets out a long, long exhalation of relief.)

Q. Show me what, Mom?

A. Just come in.

(MARK enters the ladies' room.)

Q. Where are you?

A. I'm in here.

(He walks over to a closed stall.)

Q. Hey, uh...I think I'm gonna wait outside for you, okay?

A. No, come in here. I have to show you something!

(He slowly opens the door to the stall. His mother is on her hands and knees in front of the toilet staring down at something on the floor with the intense absorption of a...a myrmecologist *examining an anthill.)*

A. Look at that.

Q. What?

(She points to a web of cracks in the tile.)

A. This face, right here. It's him!

(He squeezes in next to his mother, gets down on his hands and knees, and scrutinizes the craquelure.)

Q. Where do you see a face?

A. Right here. I think that might be the Imaginary In-tern!

Q. I don't see a face.

A. Here, sweetheart, here...these are the eyes, here's the nose...it's in sort of semi-profile.

Q. That's not the Imaginary Intern.

A. It's not? Are you sure?

Q. I'm sure.

A. I was so excited. I was sitting here and I looked down and I thought, *Oh my goodness!*

Q. Mom, how would you even know what the Imaginary Intern looks like? You've never even seen the Imaginary Intern.

A. I just had a very clear picture in my mind of what he looks like from everything you said about him.

(MARK cants his head to the side and, squinting his eyes, gives this particular configuration of cracks another appraisal.)

Q. The Imaginary Intern has a ... a fuller face. More boyish. Not so gaunt, y'know? That sort of looks like ... like ... who's that guy, that actor with the big nose?

A. Karl Malden?

Q. *(Laughing.)* No, Mom, today! He was in, uh ... he was in that movie *The Pianist* ... and, um ... what is that, uh ... *Summer of Sam.* He was in a beer commercial ... I think it was a Stella Artois commercial. God, I can picture him perfectly, and I just cannot think of his name ...

A. You know something funny? I've just never liked beer. It looks so good on a hot day...But I just never liked it.

Q. Oh, that Woody Allen movie, *Midnight in Paris*...he was in that...He played Salvador Dalí...Adrien Brody!

A. I love that movie!

Q. Did you ever see *Un Chien Andalou*? It's better.

(He sighs.)

Q. You know, you really scared the shit out of me. I didn't know what happened to you.

A. That's so silly of you. I just had to pee.

Q. You remember that poor little boy, James Bulger...that, that toddler who was kidnapped from the mall in England, and he was subsequently murdered, and the whole abduction was caught on CCTV cameras? I thought for a minute that—I don't know—I thought that...that something like that might have happened to you...but sort of inside out, y'know? Here, the mom is kidnapped and the little boy is left in the mall frantically searching for her. I even thought for a minute that those guys might have taken you.

A. What guys?

Q. The Panda Express and the Sbarro guys.

A. I'm not such a pushover, you know. I wouldn't let two guys just abscond with me like that.

Q. I was freaking, seriously. I was getting the tintinnab-ulation, the tinea versicolor, the pruritus ani...it was, like, textbook.

(MARK'S MOM is examining another pattern of cracks on the floor.)

Q. Mom, why did you stop me before? It seemed like you stopped me just as I started talking about how magnificent and loving Mercedes was when she took care of me.

A. *(Without looking up from the craquelure.)* I just didn't want to hear any more.

Q. About Mercedes?

A. No, no, no...About you being sick, and about you being in so much discomfort and feeling

221

so ... so undignified. I just couldn't ... I just couldn't stand it.

(She looks at him.)

A. You know, when you were diagnosed, when you told me ... I was terror-stricken ... so that I forced myself, I suppose, not really to think about it deeply. But it changed my whole life. It changed the things I thought about before I went to sleep certainly ... every single bloody night. And I ... I faced the knowledge that something awful might happen by not facing the knowledge, if that makes any sense at all. By knowing it and trying very hard to set it back one level, so that I could keep going and not show you that I was frightened. And I kept thinking this thing that might make no kind of sense, as we're talking about this—I kept thinking that if there were only some way I could make it be me and not you ... Because parents should die and not their children. And I still feel the same way. I want to be the first to go ... and leave everybody happy, healthy, and in wonderful shape. I'd also like to leave all of you rich if I could, but I haven't figured that one out yet.

(Returning her attention to the floor, she continues.)

A. Is this video game you were talking about ... is it like a suicide?

Q. No, no...it's like the story of a son umbilicated to his mother, a son moored in port. The "death" should be read figuratively—it's a heaving up of the anchor. Freud talked about how the human body longs to return to the indeterminacy of the inorganic...about an urge in organic life to restore an earlier state of things. That's sort of what I was trying to get at, I guess.

A. It almost seems like overkill to me.

Q. What do you mean?

A. Well, there's a mall shooter, there's a flood, there's going back into a mother's womb and unraveling the father's and mother's DNA in the zygote...

Q. A couple of years ago, I read an article about a woman named Cecilia Chang, a dean and a fundraiser at St. John's University, who was involved in this, this huge fraud and corruption scandal. And toward the end of her trial, less than twenty-four hours after testifying, convinced that she was going to be convicted, she committed suicide at her home in, uh...in Queens. She started a fire in her bedroom fireplace and closed the flue. She went downstairs to the kitchen and turned on the gas. She slit her wrists. And then she hanged herself with stereo speaker wire from a lowered attic ladder. And I remember thinking, *Fuck, this woman was not leaving anything to chance!* So, I think that was probably the inspiration for that...y'know, that re-dundancy in the game.

A. Did you really ask the surgeon to look in my brain and see why I talk so much?

Q. I have to think there's a correlation between hyper-emesis gravidarum and projectile logorrhea. And I really do believe that there's a genetic link between a mother's pathologically excessive talkativeness and a son's persistent fantasy of gesticulating from a balcony and haranguing a crowd in a piazza. Don't you?

A. Well, as long as you brought up Freud...I think we need to ask two psychoanalytical questions here: What does the form of this autobiography dis-place, repress, or disavow? And what is striking in its absence here? What is being occluded? Be-cause, doesn't the real story always consist of the very content that's being occluded?

Q. Look, all I know is that everyone, at one point in his or her life, has had to suck some microcephalic moron's dick for cab fare, figuratively speaking, of course...But it just seems to be getting harder and harder for me as I get older.

(She reaches up behind her, tears off a few sheets of toilet paper, and wipes some grime off another pattern on the tile.)

A. What time is Mussolini picking you up?

Q. Very funny.

A. You said it was like a flight-simulation game, right?

Q. Yeah.

A. Well, when you play, where can you go? Where can you go in the flying balcony?

Q. Well initially you just sort of fly around here...so I was thinking, like, y'know, Paramus, Mahwah, Ramsey, Wayne, uh...Hackensack.

A. That doesn't seem like such a great a game to me.

Q. Well, Mom, that would just be like the first level. And also, you've got to keep in mind that you're...well, you're not "dead" exactly, but the psychophysical aggregate that was "you" has dis-aggregated.

A. You know something that occurred to me when you were talking before? I think you're too hard on yourself about your father.

225

Q. No, I'm too impatient with him. I'm an impatient person. There's a blind guy who works out at my gym, and the other day he passed gas. And it was pretty loud. And, my immediate reaction was like, *Eww,* dude, gross...but then I thought that the farting is probably some kind of echolocation technique that the guy is using so he can navigate around the gym...which would be really cool, y'know? But my first reaction, my sort of default response was just this kind of impatient judgment without taking the time to try and understand what was going on...

(MARK'S MOM points to another indeterminate visage on the floor.)

A. You know who that looks like a little bit?

Q. I think that looks a little like Julianne Moore...if Julianne Moore had cystic acne or something.

A. Where are you looking?

Q. Over here.

A. No, Mark—here, *here.* Tell me who *that* looks like to you. You see where I'm talking about? Here— there's a head and the neck...

Q. Are you talking about that guy who does the show

226

on the Food Network? You think it looks like *that*
guy?

A. What guy?

Q. The guy who hosts that show where they give you
the different foods and you have to combine them
somehow into a meal...like Arctic char, goji
berries, mascarpone cheese, and cotton
candy...*Chopped*. The host of *Chopped*. You think
that looks like the host of *Chopped*?

A. No, no, no. It looks like that lovely Italian anesthesiologist I was talking about before, remember? The
one that made a pass at me when I was pregnant
with you.

Q. Mom, how could I possibly recognize someone who
made a pass at you when you were pregnant with
me? What did I have, like intrauterine X-ray vision or something? You wanna know who that
actually looks like to me now? Remember I took
you to that incredibly brutal, gory Korean movie?
Uh, what was that called? Uh...*I Saw the Devil*.
Remember that? And you walked out.

A. Oh God, yes! Why did you take me to something
like that?

MARK LEYNER

Q. Mom, when I suggested it, you told me you'd read
   about it in the *Times* and wanted to go see it with
   me.

A. I must have gotten it mixed up with something else.

Q. Well, anyway—it sort of looks like the guy who
   played the serial killer...uh...Choi Min-sik.

(She shrugs.)

A. You know I wanted to ask you something—you
   mentioned a couple of times what if someone
   asked you to give advice to young writers, but you
   never really gave a straight answer. Do you actually have any advice you'd give?

Q. Well, you know what?...Seriously...this is a
   straight answer...and I think this is true for everyone, and so logically it must be true for young
   writers: never eat candy out of those, those open
   bins they have in the lobbies of movie theaters. I
   went to this multiplex once to see, uh...I don't remember what I was seeing...but, I was in the
   men's room before the movie started, and I
   watched this guy come out of a...a stall, and not
   wash his hands, and he heads straight for those
   candy bins in the lobby, and he sticks his gross, un-
   washed, *E. coli* hand in this bin of sour gummy

228

worms or whatever it was and rummages the fuck around in there. I mean, that's like direct ass-to-mouth candy. (That's a...a porn expression. You probably don't know that one...)

A. That's absolutely revolting.

Q. Well, y'know, aphids drink leaf sap and then excrete droplets of this sugary liquid from their rear ends, and that's the stuff that ants drink, so...I mean, it does happen in nature.

(He shrugs, changing the subject.)

Q. What would you say if someone said to me, "I don't think there was any reading. I don't think there's any autobiography. I don't think there's any fuck-ing, uh...any fucking video game. I think you and your mom just came to a mall, came to a food court, sat down, and had something to eat. And I think you just stood up on a table and started talk-ing like some fucking nutjob. Or did some kind of loony reenactment of your internal psychodramas or you and your mother's weird-ass folie à deux, or some reenactment of your little...your weird little lunches together at the Bird Cage at Lord & Tay-lor a million years ago. And that's *all* this whole thing is." What would you say to that?

A. You know what I'd say? I'd say, that's the great thing about literature. Everyone's entitled to his or her own interpretation. *That's* what I'd say to that.

Q. Well, all I know is—I'm "real." I'm bringing "realness." I'm singing all the parts. And if the flying balcony with Mussolini at the helm turns out to be a bathroom stall with my mom, then so be it. If being on my hands and my knees, wedged in this stall forever with my mom, if that turns out to be my version of that cell, that birdcage in *King Lear*, and if this sort of, this sort of... of contrapuntal chirping is what we end up doing forever, sort of gently batting our minds' eyeballs back and forth and back and forth like, like feathered shuttlecocks... if we're just these two incessantly twittering birds, these two little winged larynxes flying around each other in a birdcage... like those motorcyclists, those stunt riders who race around each other in those mesh spheres, in those "globes of death" at circuses, at carnivals, like, uh... like, uh, Ryan Gosling in that movie *The Place Beyond the Pines*. If it turns out that's all this whole thing is... then so be it. You know?

(MARK'S MOM recognizes someone new in yet another configuration of cracks on the floor.)

A. Well, for God's sake!

Q. What?

A. When we moved to West Orange, I guess I was
looking for a store where I could have a...a personal sort of relationship, the way I did in Jersey
City...and, um, there was this place called
Rolli's or Rolli's Market that had been recom-
mended to me possibly, probably by Judy
Leiberman, or by other people in the neighborhood who said that their butcher shop was very,
very good, and that's how I started to use them.
And *that*—right over there—that looks to me,
that looks uncannily to me like Joe Rolli. Joe's
brother—whose name I'm trying to remember
as I'm speaking to you—his older brother was
the butcher. And the quality of the meat he carried and his ability to cut the meat, to prepare it
properly, was wonderful, and they delivered as
well. So sometimes I would just call in to them
and order a roast and, uh...they'd deliver, and
sometimes as I developed the habit, as I became
used to driving in the neighborhood more, of
driving down the hill and stopping there en
route to wherever I was going, I'd get a grocery
order as well. And the younger brother—a sort
of ruddy-cheeked, round-faced nice guy—was
Joe...that was the...he was in charge of the
grocery department. And they were, uh, very,
very, very nice to me and always had time to

talk, and, if anything turned out to be not perfect, they would see to it...they would give me another one, a better one. And they'd ask after the family, and it just became this very warm and comfortable and comforting kind of arrangement, which doesn't mean certainly that I didn't go to Kings Market, because I did, constantly, but rather than use the meat department at Kings, I, uh...I used Rolli's as long as I lived in West Orange. There were other places too, and you know I'm a champion food buyer, so if we wanted to have a certain kind of thing, I would go to that kind of place...like, if we wanted fried chicken, barbecued chicken, or one of the other specialties, I'd go to the place called the Chicken Nest and shop there, um...now the original Chicken Nest was...all right, now I'm going to forget the names of some of the streets? The street that runs parallel to, uh, Wyoming... to Gregory...um...below it...where, when we moved to Maplewood, Chase's school was on that street...

Q. Valley?

A. Valley, yes. So you'd drive down to Valley, and then you'd make a turn one block further south down the hill, and there was the little tiny parking lot and, um, the Chicken Nest. And they came to

know me...they'd say, "Hello, Mrs. Leyner!" and,
uh...you went to summer camp with one of their
children, one of the owner's children...

Q. Oh, that's right. I remember...I remember him.

A. And you could get all kinds of poultry there, and
you could get chicken soups, and their potato
salad was great, and on holidays, and maybe other
times too, they had, um...yams. Do you remember the yams from there? Your sister adored them.
They were mashed yams and they were wonderful,
and they also had, uh...people in those days used
as side dishes, things like a cranberry mold or a,
uh, uh...there was one mold that looked like
green Jell-O.

Q. Oh yeah. What was in that green Jell-O mold?

A. They must have put either cottage cheese or, uh,
cream cheese, and then pulverized it, so it was that
lovely sort of lime-green color. It was a lime mold
and it had, I think, some pineapple in it as
well...And they also barbecued chickens and barbecued ducks...you could get ducks quartered.
And I used to take those, those ducks, and cook
them again with a sauce like a...like a cherry
sauce or an orange Grand Marnier sauce for en-
tertaining...because then they were nice and

tender on the inside and extra-crispy on the outside, but I didn't have to put up with all the fat
from cooking duck from the beginning. So there
were lots of specialty stores—Jewish delicatessens
where you could get lox and bagels—and I used
all of them...but my go-to people if I was either in
a hurry or somebody wasn't feeling well and we
couldn't go out or just because it was comfortable
and warm, I would use the Rolli brothers. And
when I moved away from West Orange, and then
even when I sold the house in Maplewood and
moved away, I would get an occasional call...in
the beginning it was fairly frequent, and after a
while sometimes it would be like even once a
year...and it would be Joe. And he'd say, "I was
thinking about you. I was thinking about your
great smile. I was thinking about..."—it was
funny because he'd say "your beautiful blue eyes."
Well, he might have liked them, but they're not
blue. They're green, and they're still green. Never-
theless, I thought it was very funny and very
cute...I learned a little bit about his family...I
think I learned more about his family after the
fact, y'know, when he used to make these calls. It
turned out that one of his children, one of his
daughters, married the man who became gover-
nor for a while in New Jersey...um, took over the
governorship...I'm not even sure...was that
when McGreevey had to leave or resign?

Q. Oh, this was recent?

A. Yeah...But I know...I can't remember his
   name...but he's still in government, Joe's son-in-
   law. So...they both had nice families, they were
   nice men...the place was as clean as could
   be...and, uh, it's the kind of shopping, the kind of
   transaction that I used to watch, I now realize, my
   mother make all the time...She'd walk on Jackson
   Avenue in Jersey City and go to her greengrocer
   and go to her butcher and stop and pass the time
   of day with all the other people. They knew her
   well, she knew them. They knew all about our
   family, we knew, a little less I would think, about
   their families...but enough to ask how their son
   was doing in medical school, and so on and so
   forth...and it was that very human contact, I
   think, that I learned from my mom, and that,
   without realizing it at the time, was so important
   to me and, in fact, is still important to me. I guess
   in my dealings with markets, I'll find one that has
   good-quality things but also gives that feeling...that if I really needed something on a dark
   and snowy night, they'd bring it over. Just as the
   nice young man over at Palisade Bagel...when it
   first opened...a Korean mother and son...for all
   I know they own lots of other things too...but I
   could see how hard they were working and it
   wasn't busy in the beginning, at all...all the

people in the high-rise buildings, I'm sure they
raised an eyebrow and said, sort of, Show me that
you know what this stuff is, what do *you* know
about this? And I went in and saw this woman
who rarely smiles...who gives this very minimal
little smile...and I watched her interaction with
her son, who is *very* American and is as nice a boy
as you could meet...and if the subject ever came
up or if it was possible for me to say to people,
Y'know I was just across the street at the
market—I would say as I was coming up from the
downstairs hallway, or in the elevator—and the
things they have are really excellent, their bagels
are really good bagels and the tuna salad is the
best tuna salad, and your sister calls me from Wee-
hawken about buying tuna salad and bringing it
over to her—that's how good it is. My fussy, fussy
daughter. I mean, I'm not claiming that I made
their success—that would be rather self-
aggrandizing and I don't mean that...but I think
that they understood, and I think they understood
very early on...and the son in particular...I
could see that when I got home, that there was an
extra bagel thrown in, or if they were covering
everything up and closing up...I always used to
forget that they closed at four thirty...that he
would wait and unlock the door for me and say,
"Don't you worry, Mrs. Leyner, it's no problem at
all." And it's really lovely, it's really nice to have

that, and, uh...I've called once or twice...I called
when I had the flu a couple of years ago, I called
when I had the bursitis in my hip and I wasn't supposed to move around...and I would say who I
was and ask if it would be possible for someone to
bring something over...and they'd say, "Of
course!" And maybe they do that for everybody,
but it's the feeling I like and the feeling I have with
them...and it's very nice. So, I think I automati-
cally end up trying to re-create that kind of thing
for myself. You remember...I don't know if you
do...that we had what they called a chicken-and-
egg man who used to deliver to us in Jersey City.
From Lakewood. He used to come in his little
truck.

Q. Where's Lakewood?

A. Lakewood is near the seashore. And at this point in
    time it has, I think, an enormous, very, very ortho-
    dox Jewish community. There are many, many
    very orthodox young families...a young woman
    who looks like she can't be more than twenty-five
    or twenty-eight years old with about five or six
    children and pregnant again...But it was always
    known as a rural, farming area, where, uh, eggs,
    butter...I used to buy sweet butter from him,
    fresh eggs and chicken. And one day your dog,
    Shadow, almost ate him alive.

Q. What happened?

A. I had Shadow on the leash...on Westminster
Lane...when I had walked out the front door just
as his little panel truck pulled up, and he asked
what I wanted and I told him, and we talked
about one thing or another—I don't remember
what it was—and he started to explain something
to me and he went like *this,* in explanation, he sort
of put his arm out, "Well, you know, you know
how that is"...as he did that, the dog, being as
overly protective as he was, he threw his body
through the hedge that was in front of the house,
rammed right through the hedge, snapping his
teeth and growling, and this poor young man just
about got into the truck and slid the panel closed
before he had something bitten off. But, yeah...he
used to come a couple of times a week, and that
was terrific. And I probably learned about him
through my mom, who was the world's champion
at all of this kind of thing.

Q. Did you know that bats' laryngeal muscles can con-
tract up to two hundred times per second?

A. No, I didn't know that.

Q. Y'know, you did such an incredible job reading that
MMPI report, that, uh...that Minnesota Mul-

tiphasic Personality Inventory report, that we
probably should have just planned on letting you
do the whole reading. I probably should have just
stayed away altogether.

A. Oh, that's ridiculous, Mark.

Q. No, seriously, I should have. It reminds me a little of
that story about the conceptual artist... Do you
know that story?

A. I don't think so.

Q. There was this conceptual artist, this very brilliant,
very enigmatic, intransigent, reclusive artist. And he
was doing this, this astonishing project... it was
called something like, uh, *Outside-In* ... and it involved putting everything outside of the Whitney
into the Whitney (this was the new Whitney down
in Meatpacking). And by everything, I mean *everything* and *everyone*—the Pacific Ocean, the Alps, the
Burj Khalifa, the Kurdish Peshmerga, the Pitts-
burgh Penguins, every single can of corned-beef
hash and SpaghettiOs, every Depeche Mode CD,
every Pole, Turk, and Inuit, every chicken, bear, water moccasin, tomahawk missile, Uber car,
umbrella, iPhone, and flushable wipe, every canister
of nerve gas and bottle of beer—every single thing
and every single person on earth (including every

other piece of art in the world too, of course, as well as a scale model of the museum and all its contents). It was without a doubt the most challenging installation the Whitney had ever mounted, costing, like, trillions upon trillions of dollars for insurance and shipping, with crews working seven days a week in eleven-hour shifts. And so...finally...this remarkable show opens. And everything and everyone in the world is in the Whitney Museum...Or so we think. Until a small child, a small, chubby naive child, looks up at his dad, tugging at his pants leg, and asks, "Where's the artist?" Well...the artist—the great artist—out of shyness or modesty or perhaps out of a sense of superiority, an aristocratic de haut en bas disdain, has apparently refused to attend his own opening, fatally undermining the conceptual integrity of the entire project. And everything is removed and everyone sullenly files out, muttering to themselves, until the museum is completely empty...and the everything-and-everyone-in-the-world that was once *inside* the Whitney is now *outside* the Whitney.

A. That sounds like one of those folktales I used to read to you while you were eating.

(MARK is gazing at his MOM, who's gazing down at the floor again.)

Q. There's a beautiful cliff behind the Walgreen's on

River Road in North Bergen...I was hoping maybe we'd get our picture taken there. The bush clover is splendid this time of year.

(For a moment, they both seem lost in their own reveries.)

Q. I want to take a picture of us, okay?

(He tries to stand so he can reach into his pants pocket and get his phone.)

Q. We're kind of wedged in here...

A. Do you want me to...

Q. I think I can reach it without having to get up...

A. Should I...

Q. Got it.

(He holds the phone out in front of them, having to extend his arm out over the threshold of the stall in order to fit them both in the frame.)

Q. Ready?

A. Not really.

Q. Smile...

(We hear the cell-phone shutter click.)

A. I must look like a gargoyle.

Q. You look beautiful, Mom. Do you remember that story in the news about that North Korean general, Hyon Yong-chol...the one Kim Jong-un supposedly ordered executed by antiaircraft gun? I tweeted something like, uh...*Being executed with an antiaircraft gun doesn't seem like such a bad way to go. Beats becoming one of those "Fifteen Celebs Who Are Aging Horribly."* Well...you're aging remarkably, *miraculously*...You know, I realized something tonight that I never ever realized before...I think we have a—what would you call it?—a shared expressivity, a shared expressivity both in terms of its sheer volume and its style...There's like a...an *isomorphism* between the way you express yourself and the way I do...And, honestly, that's something I don't think ever occurred to me before tonight.

A. That's such a wonderful, unexpected thing for you to say.

Q. Who are your favorite mother/son duos? Like in mythology or literature and history?

(MARK'S MOM is surveying the craquelure, trying to discern one last face.)

A. Oh, I don't know, sweetheart. Who are yours?

242

Q. I guess Jocasta and Oedipus, and Ma and "Doc"
     Barker and, uh...maybe Cher and Chaz Bono.

A. Okay...I might be going completely crazy
     here...but tell me that's not Elston Howard.

Q. Elston Howard?

A. Yes...the catcher for the Yankees back in the, in
     the sixties.

Q. Where do you see Elston Howard?

A. Right over here...God, I used to love watching
     him. I love watching catchers anyway. And even
     before I really understood—I was young and it
     didn't even occur to me very much—but the pain
     that they must be in virtually all the time, oh my
     Lord! To be in that position...It's got to be devas-
     tating to your knees and hips.

Q. The position we're in right now couldn't be that
     great for our knees and hips...

A. He lived in Teaneck, y'know—Elston Howard.
     That's another thing I've learned in my age now,
     now that I live in Bergen County...so many of the
     players, even now, live in Bergen County. The
     great CC lives close by...CC Sabathia lives close

by, and his wife, Amber, is in lots and lots of charity events and things...

Q. They live in Fort Lee?

A. They might live in Tenafly...they live in one of
the...obviously enough, in a gorgeous home, in a
gorgeous place...it could even be Alpine or De-
marest, but it's one of the Bergen County
places...My father, Raymond, by the way, liked
baseball very much, of course, but he *loved* tennis,
and he was quite a good tennis player, you know.
Of course, anything *you* did, especially if you did it
well—and you did most things well—he was just
so proud of you that his chest, which stuck way out
anyway, almost broke off from glee...

(Water is beginning to seep into the bathroom and pool on the floor.

The lights begin to flicker and dim.)

A. The image I have in my mind when I think of you and
my dad is always the one of him taking you for a
walk when you were very little, and you're holding
on to, I think, one of his fingers, and he's walking
with his chest way, way out. He's so thrilled with "his
boy." You were his first boy. And *what* a boy...

(And finally the lights go out.)

PART IV

ADJOURNMENT

*(When the lights come back on, we are in the corridor outside the ladies'
room.*

The door is closed.

We hear the two of them still speaking from within . . .

*And, after several moments, LEYNER emerges, in a bathrobe, flushed
from the exertion of the performance, his hair slicked back, daubs of cold
cream dappling his face, like an actor who's hurriedly refreshed himself
in his dressing room before returning for a curtain call.*

*A deep breath and a long, sighing, exhausted, but gratified exhalation,
and then a wide grin — an implicit "I'm getting too old for this."*

*LEYNER is, of course, the same person as MARK [the former, in fact,
merely the surname of the latter], and yet he seems distinctly different from
the one wedged in that tiny stall with his mother, almost as if he's somehow*

left him behind in there. [One can almost picture the two of them still in there, on their hands and knees, parsing the craquelure, interpreting their hieroglyphs . . . almost still discern the decrescendo of their everlasting repartee.] Clearly spent from the rigors of his role tonight, he now seems less fraught, unburdened somehow, more relaxed, ever so slightly out of character, even if this just means a self-awareness, a . . . a disengagement, a divestiture of one self to disclose a virtually identical self beneath.)

LEYNER

When I was a little boy, sometimes I used to stay over on Saturday nights at my grandparents' apartment, these were my dad's parents, Sam and Rose . . . this little, one-bedroom, one-bathroom apartment over on Gifford Avenue and the Boulevard in Jersey City. And we'd all watch *The Jackie Gleason Show* together, one of the incarnations of the variety show he used to do for CBS in the sixties, the one with the June Taylor Dancers and Sammy Spear and His Orchestra and Frank Fontaine. And Gleason used to come back out on stage at the end of the show, in his bathrobe, and address the audience and sometimes bring some of the cast members out for curtain calls. And he'd seem spent, but so happily, so exuberantly spent, if that makes any sense . . . which is just the way I feel right now, right here, tonight.

When my grandfather Sam was in his mid-seventies, he developed leukemia, and he endured several terribly arduous years with the disease . . . he developed sores in his mouth that were excruciatingly painful and made it very difficult for him to eat just about anything that he liked, he was exhausted, debilitated, homebound for the most part. It was a difficult time, a grim time for him. And then one day—so I remember it—he seemed to spontaneously recover. He woke up with terrific energy and high spirits…And that evening, he got dressed up (he'd always been quite a dandy, quite a clotheshorse), picked out one of his fancy walking sticks, got in his car (he'd always loved driving, loved his flying balcony), and he took my grandma Rose to some restaurant down on the Jersey shore that they both loved, and they had a fabulous lobster dinner. And he died in his sleep early the next morning.

I was talking to Rose once—I don't remember if it was when she was living in her apartment in Florida or if it was when she was in that assisted-living facility in, uh…in the Valley, in LA—and I was talking about some particular married couple and whether they were happy or not, and Rose said with this very memorable kind of disdain and incredulity, "*Happy?* Do you think your grandfather and I were *happy?*" I don't think she meant to imply that she and my grandfather were *miserable* in any way, it was just that word *happy* that she seemed to find so patently inappropriate, because, I think, in her mind it implied this sort of blithe fantasy world, when, in reality—and I'm putting words in her mouth here—an enduring marriage requires a hard-won and often begrudging modus vivendi. I don't think she meant any of this in an especially cynical way, and

I'm fairly certain most other women her age, and of her generation, would have said basically the same thing. Although Rose did frequently add that all men were snakes. But she'd say even that with a smile and her Betty Boop blink-blink-blink. And then she'd look at me and say, "He was such a handsome man...I miss him." Blink-blink-blink.

Well...I miss him too. And I miss you, Rose...and I miss Ray and Harriet, and all those wonderful, inimitable people from that time. And I miss that whole world, with its lulling strobe of passing verdant days, the pointillist haze of its afternoons, with all its rooms and murmuring voices. That has all disappeared forever...

(He shrugs and sighs, and smiles.)

LEYNER

I want to express my immense gratitude to my mom.

When I first asked her if she'd like to do this...to sit with me and let me interview her and use the transcripts in this book...she said, "Oh, honey, I don't know if I could do that. I'd be so self-conscious. I'd almost feel as if I were playing myself." And I said, "Of course you can do it. You'll be great." I said, "Look at all these silly people...these, these silly reality stars, all these buxom socialites and degenerate hillbillies, these lonesome dwarfs and hoarders. You'll be absolutely fantastic."

And even though she's never watched *any* of these kinds of shows, she's never even seen a single episode of *Keeping Up with the Kardashians* or the *Real Housewives* of This or That, never mind anything like *Wives with Knives* or *Sex Sent Me to the Slammer* or anything of that ilk—she's much more of a *Downton Abbey / Inspector Morse* kind of person—she acquiesced, and she was, as she has always, *always* been, so beautifully astute and insightful and eloquent and, as I predicted, just absolutely fantastic.

But the main reason that I came out here is to thank *you.*

You know, Jackie Gleason used to end his variety show bellowing, "Miami Beach audiences are the greatest audiences in the world!" Well, we're not in Miami Beach...and I'm not much of a bellower now, if I ever was, but...you are the greatest too. You really are. The hours you spent reading this really do represent an irrevocable loss for you. You can never get that time back. That part of your life is gone forever. I'm profoundly grateful to you for that.

And so with this, I say good-bye to you, a very real good-bye:

I am going west, to better secure material subsistence for my family and myself.

I have released my mind, after almost sixty years of loyal service.

I can only hope it will find its way back to its primordial home, which it left so long ago.

Moushiwake gozaimasen deshita.

ABOUT THE AUTHOR

Mark Leyner is the author of the novels *The Sugar Frosted Nutsack; My Cousin, My Gastroenterologist; Et Tu, Babe;* and *The Tetherballs of Bougainville.* His nonfiction includes the #1 *New York Times* bestseller *Why Do Men Have Nipples?* Leyner cowrote the movie *War, Inc.* He currently lives in Hoboken, New Jersey.